What About Me?

Colby Rodowsky

What About Me?

A Sunburst Book

Farrar, Straus & Giroux

For Sister Maura

What About Me?

1

It's hard to hate your brother.

Not actually doing it. I don't mean that. From what I understand, everyday garden-variety brothers can drive you right up a wall, what with their dirty gym socks, and insects stored in pill bottles all over the place, and the things they say into the phone—especially when the call's not even for them.

But that deep-down feeling of absolutely, positively not being able to stand someone—that's hard. It takes a lot out of you. It sometimes makes me think of a hamster going around and around on one of those wheels—you can't stop, but you never get anywhere.

It's the kind of thing I think about a lot, in the middle of the night, or the middle of the middle of things. One of those times when everybody stops talking and you can hear the clock tick.

Still, I wonder. About me, and Fredlet, and Mom and Dad, and Guntzie, and the spring of my sophomore year in high school. But mostly I wonder about Fredlet.

Fredlet: my brother, and that spring when I was fifteen he was eleven—except in his head he was more like three.

And I hated him.

Honest-to-God hate. Not all the time; not every day; but enough to scare me sometimes. But then other times I wanted to sit down next to him on the floor and listen to that blasted *Sesame Street* record with him, and let him show me stuff out of the Sears, Roebuck catalog; it was a 1964 catalog, but not to Fredlet. If that's not the kind of thing to make you want to throw the psych book in the incinerator and switch to typing, I don't know what is.

It had always been a sort of love-hate thing with me and Fredlet, ever since the day my mother brought him home from the hospital. I remember, because I was four and had on new Sunday shoes and I wasn't sure whether I felt all excited because of the new shoes or the baby or because my mother was coming home. I remember that my mother wasn't fat anymore and I could get my arms all the way around her waist. Mom sat down on the couch and Dad put the blue blanket thing in her arms and she said, "Look, Dorrie. Here he is. Your very own brother, Freddie."

And right then I said it. "Piglet. He looks like Piglet, Momma." It had been my sort of Winnie the Pooh period (you know, the way Picasso had his blue period), and I thought why couldn't we have a Pooh Bear baby, or even a Roo. "No, Momma. He's Piglet, Piglet, Piglet." And I stamped my foot and the new Sunday shoe sounded like a slap on the hard wood floor. Somehow I must have gotten the feeling that my mother was upset because I remember reaching out and touching the baby's cheek. "Okay, Momma. He's Fredlet, then. Poor Fredlet." And his cheek felt cool as marble.

Looking back, I guess it was his eyes that told me what I didn't know I knew, or what nobody else had even dared to think. It was always his eyes, and his tongue, and later on a lot of other things, or rather not doing a lot of other things that led to the doctors and the tests and the answers we didn't want to hear.

The words *Down's syndrome.*

My mother still can't say those words without her voice catching. *Down's syndrome.* And the school for retarded children, except that they call them exceptional children. I never really understood that. Like maybe the parents didn't know which end of "exceptional" they had.

Mom and Dad always called him Fred, but to almost everybody else—and especially to me—Fredlet never got over being Fredlet. And I loved him some and I hated him some, like a seesaw that was pretty evenly matched. Until that spring of my sophomore year, and then that seesaw really went crashing down—on the hate side. And there was love up high dangling its legs. I guess it was me—I, 'cause Fredlet was the same. He was always the same.

2

Nothing made sense any-
more. Even things that were perfectly logical didn't
make any sense at all. Like the night of the Parents'
Club Dinner-Dance at Miss Benson's School—and
my parents expecting me to baby-sit. That's reason-
able: a fifteen-year-old girl taking care of her
eleven-year-old brother. Except not on the spur of
the moment, with no warning, and when I had
something else to do. And the way my mother acted
it wasn't even important—what I had to do, I mean.

It all started when I came in from school late that
Friday afternoon. Everything smelled all lemon-
clean, and my mother was in the kitchen rolling the
cheese ball in chopped nuts, and Fredlet was on the
floor eating Saltine crackers and sitting in a mountain of crumbs that looked like snowflakes.

"Hi, Mom. Hi, Fredlet. What's going on?" I
asked.

"Hi, Dorrie. Remember, we're having a few people in for drinks before the dinner-dance, but the most terrible thing has happened. Mrs. Moran has broken her ankle. Her daughter called this morning. We really have to go to the dance, especially since we're having guests beforehand. You'll just have to help me out."

"Sure, Mom. What needs doing? Everything looks okay to me."

"I'm afraid you'll have to baby-sit with Fred for us. There's just no one else."

"Baby-sit? When? Not tonight?"

Fredlet climbed up out of his pile of Saltine crumbs. "Baby-sit. Baby-sit. Baby-sit. Dorrie baby-sit Fredlet." And he started to slide around the floor on his Indian slippers.

"Dorrie, get those crumbs up for me, please. I just vacuumed and I'm afraid Fred'll track them into the hall," said my mother.

"But, Mom, I can't baby-sit. Not tonight. I mean, I just can't. I'm going out."

"Dorrie, the crumbs. Watch out—you missed the trash can. I'm sorry, but there's no other choice. We have the tickets, we've invited company, and anyway, all your friends' parents will be there."

I swept the crumbs up again and slammed the dustpan down into the trash can.

"Mo-ther, I can't. I don't care whose parents are going. Nobody else has to baby-sit. Not tonight. I just can't."

Mom put the cheese ball in the refrigerator and

took out the sour cream to make the dip for the cauliflower and stuff. I mean, you'd think if she was going to ruin my entire social life she'd at least look at me instead of doing things in little bowls.

"Dorrie, I'm sorry, but that's the way it will have to be. We'll be in all tomorrow night. You can go out then."

"Tomorrow?" I said. "What good will that do me? There's nothing going on tomorrow night except that dumb mixer—but tonight Linda Ready's having a party. I just have to go."

Fredlet ate another handful of Saltines and Mom added dried onion soup to the sour cream.

"I can't. Not tonight—I . . ."

"Dorrie, I'm afraid there's nothing else I can do. Between you and Mrs. Moran we haven't had to use any other sitter for a long time. I just can't call an agency and get a perfect stranger in here. You know Fred isn't always the easiest child to manage. Anyway, there'll be other parties."

I really had to bite my tongue to keep from saying "There'll be other dinner-dances, too," but I thought that would be a not-too-smart thing to say. And knowing Mom, I thought it was probably not something she really wanted to do. She's not really the dinner-dance type.

"I don't care about other parties," I said, and as I said it I knew I sounded all whiny and spoiled and feel-sorry-for-yourself-ish, but I said it anyway. "I don't care about other parties. I care about this one."

My mother went on putting the dip away and wiping off the counters and the fronts of cabinets. "You'll really have to get your head out of the clouds and think about something besides yourself and your art for a change."

Why do mothers always throw things up at you when they get mad? And I could tell she was mad by the way she was wiping those cabinets. I mean, most of the time Mom's glad I like art because she did too, once, a long time ago, before she decided to make a career of Fredlet.

But to get back to the art. I have this thing for it. I always have had, sort of. I don't mean just looking at it but doing it, with my hands. Anything: pencils, charcoal, pastels. But right then mostly it was clay. I guess I had Guntzie to thank for the ceramics bit. Guntzie was our neighbor and friend and my art teacher at Miss Benson's. But she was my teacher because she was our friend first, and that helped make up my parents' minds to send me to Miss Benson's. That and the fact that it was only three blocks away.

For a while I had this idea about going to New Mexico and making pots and selling them by the side of the road and living off the land and all. But Guntzie thought that was a bit unstructured. Guntzie, being a free spirit and her own woman and all, keeps saying, "Art is discipline—art is discipline," over and over. Maybe that's why she is somebody.

And Guntzie really is somebody. She's listed in *Who's Who Among American Women* and has paintings in the Museum of Modern Art and all kinds of other places. Guntzie's really done a lot for Miss Benson's too. She was the one, years ago, who got the Spring Festival started. And now that's the absolutely most important thing of the whole year. And the art show's the most important part of the festival. Last year a photographer even came and there was a bunch of pictures in the Sunday *Times*.

Guntzie doesn't even have to teach at Miss Benson's, except that she says that's her contact with reality—what keeps her from being a complete loner. And anyway it's a good excuse when she doesn't want to do things like talk to fat clubwomen over creamed chicken.

Well, by this time my mother had polished every surface in the kitchen, including the bottoms of Fredlet's slippers, and had swept up his new pile of cracker crumbs—and the atmosphere was decidedly cold. But as a matter of principle I couldn't just give in without one last stand.

"Art's got nothing to do with anything, and my head's not in the clouds, and besides, I don't know what I'm going to tell Linda about her party for Pete's sake."

"Tell her you can't come because you have to baby-sit. That's easy," said Mom. "Oh, and would you see that Fred gets cleaned up and dressed. I have his clothes out on his bed. And then you can get dressed. I'm going to get a quick bath. Your father will be home any minute."

Supposedly Fredlet could dress himself. It was the kind of thing they taught him over and over at Bell-ringers School. Every time a "report card" came home, the teacher (whoever she happened to be that year) always wrote, "Fred is making progress in learning to dress himself." But just be in a hurry someday and try to get him to do it. Hah. By the time I got him out of his school clothes and sort of sponge-bathed he was really hyper. He kept saying, "Company come, Dorrie. Company for Fredlet. Party. Party. Party." And climbing up on his little step stool (he looked like a circus elephant on one of those little round steps), and jumping off. By that time he was panting so much I had to push him down on the bed. Every time I tried to grab his arms and stuff them into his shirt sleeves, his arms turned into wet noodles and sort of folded up. And then Fredlet just laughed and laughed his funny all-the-way-down-from-the-belly laugh that half the time makes me want to laugh too. That night I did—and we both sat on Fredlet's red shag rug and laughed while I tried to button his shirt and Fredlet kept saying, "Party—party—party." That's the thing about Fredlet. I can absolutely loathe him one minute, and then he'll do something—maybe just like laugh—and then I have to love him—for a while anyway.

By then Dad was home and showered and dressed,

and Mom was in her long dress and back in the kitchen putting the cheese ball on a silver tray, and I just had time to get out of my uniform and into a pair of corduroys and a shirt.

Every time the buzzer from downstairs rang, Fredlet ran for the door (except what Fredlet did was never exactly like running), and then he went out in the hall and waited by the elevator. As soon as the elevator door opened he bowed and held out his arms. He was holding his arms out for hats and coats but a lot of people didn't know that. After the first couple came, Fredlet started tugging on sleeves and stoles right there in the hall. Every time he got a coat he hugged it to him and galumped back inside and put the coats and stuff on my parents' bed. My mother's idea of a few people was actually nineteen so Fredlet had a lot of work to do. By about the third trip he was really huffing, but then, luckily, four couples arrived at the same time. And one man had a hat—that made Fredlet act like it was Christmas and Fourth of July all at once.

Fredlet put the hat on his head and went through the whole party shaking hands and stuffing cauliflower into the dip and then into his mouth. And Fredlet didn't even like cauliflower. And all around me I could hear people saying:

"Isn't he cute?"

"That type of child really is lovable."

"My, Elizabeth and Joe have done a marvelous job with him."

"And he's not a bit shy."

Even the man who owned the hat was smiling—and it was his hat that got onion dip on it every time Fredlet touched it.

The only person who wasn't being absolutely sickening about him was Guntzie. Maybe that was part of the reason I liked Guntzie so much. It wasn't that she didn't like Fredlet—she just wasn't the kind to go around fussing over someone for no reason. But then, Guntzie wasn't the type to fuss. On one of those rare times when she talked about herself, I remember her saying, "There's a lot of the mountains in me yet. Mountain people grow up learning to stand alone. It's bred into them, I guess." And the funny thing was that whenever Guntzie talked about the mountains her voice took on an almost gentle singsong quality. But what was even funnier was that Guntzie sometimes talked about the mountains. But she never went back.

Anyway, there was Guntzie looking really out of place in a black crepe dinner dress that had to have been around for at least the last ten Parents' Club dinner-dances. (Miss Benson's has mostly the kind of parents who expect teachers to show up for functions—Guntzie doesn't always make it.) Anyway, there she was nodding vaguely at a man who kept throwing out terms like "surrealist" and "cubism." And she kept looking at the door, and I could tell right off that Guntzie would rather do anything than go to the dance.

And all the time I might as well have been a sofa cushion for all the noticing I got.

By the time Fredlet made his second circuit of the living room still wearing Mr. Drew's hat, Guntzie broke away and took him by the arm and walked him into the bedroom.

"Okay, Fredlet. That's enough. Put Mr. Drew's hat down now," she said. And almost before he knew what had happened, Fredlet was back in the living room without the hat.

Maybe we should have let him keep the hat.

My father was fixing another round of drinks and my mother was putting more crackers around the cheese and looking at her watch and trying to catch Dad's eye. And there was Fredlet with nothing to do. He squatted on the floor by the coffee table and stuffed some more cauliflower and licked his fingers and then licked his hands and then his face as far as his tongue would go. That was enough to make you lose your appetite, but my mother didn't seem to notice and Dad was talking to the hat owner.

"Fredlet. Hey, Fredlet," I whispered, "get away from the table. Come here, Fredlet."

But Fredlet just kept squatting there and rocking back and forth in that funny way of his. I guess he'd had enough cauliflower—or maybe he'd eaten it all —I'm not sure, but suddenly he stood up and grabbed the tray with the cheese ball on it and lunged across the room saying, "Party—party—party—ball."

"Fredlet," I yelled, "put that down." And I made

a dive for him. The crackers flew in nine hundred directions, and the cheese ball hit the floor with a solid splat right at the feet of an overripe blonde in a Miss Teen-Age America dress.

For the next few minutes everybody crawled around on the floor looking for crackers, and Guntzie scraped up the cheese with the back of a copy of a *New Yorker* magazine. Mom kept saying, "Leave it, everybody—Dorrie'll clean it up after we leave," and then she hissed at me, "Why couldn't you have left him alone. He never would have dropped it if you hadn't yelled."

All the while Fredlet sat on an ottoman in the corner holding his stomach and rocking back and forth while Miss Teen-Age America patted his head and cooed, "Don't worry, dear boy."

And Fredlet didn't even know how to worry.

3

Well, that really cleared the party out fast. All of a sudden, people started looking at their watches and finding coats, and several of the men went down to look for taxis. Guntzie looked at me and rolled her eyes and squeezed my hand as she went out.

"You will take care of him, won't you, Dorrie?" asked my mother for about the seventeenth time.

"The phone number's over the phone, Dorrie," my father said. "But we won't be late."

"Oh," my mother went on, "do you mind terribly cleaning up these few glasses and things? The dinner starts at seven and we'll just make it. Oh, Joe, maybe we should stay home. We don't have to go, and Fred's a little keyed up tonight."

"Elizabeth, come on," said Dad from the elevator door. "Everything will be fine."

"Well, we won't be long. We may even leave right after the dinner."

Finally the door closed and I went back in and looked at the mess. Those few glasses were everywhere, and the dip was caking on the inside of the bowl, and someone had left a cigar smoldering in an ashtray.

Fredlet sat on the floor in the corner of the living room with his head on the ottoman. I tiptoed back and forth to the dishwasher hoping he would go to sleep.

By the time the place was cleaned up I was feeling pretty Cinderella-ish. The night was already ruined, so I figured I might as well ruin it all the way. I had this humungous piece of clay I'd gotten from Guntzie's apartment downstairs that needed to be wedged. And that's a really sloppy, messy, repulsive job. But you don't exactly have to be a Rhodes Scholar to do it. So I figured I could wedge the clay and take care of Fredlet at the same time. He was asleep, anyhow.

That's when Fredlet woke up.

"Me—me—me. Fredlet wants clay. Me, Dorrie. Me," he kept rattling over and over in that really foghorn voice of his.

"Aw, come on, Fredlet. Let me get this done. It's for school." Well, I should have had more sense. I could have been speaking Greek or something.

Fredlet crept closer and closer to the table, just watching and sighing a lot. Before I knew what was happening, he grabbed a whole chunk of clay. "Mine. Mine. Fredlet has clay. Make Poor Cat, like

Dorrie." He stood squeezing his white pudgy fingers into the clay.

"Fredlet Shafer. Give me that clay. Right this minute." I could have bitten my tongue as soon as I said it. That just wasn't the way to talk to Fredlet. Not if you wanted him to do anything.

"Mine. Mine," he whispered in a voice so hoarse and low I could hardly hear him. "Mine. Poor Cat," and he clutched that clay to his chest, smearing it all over his shirt and everything.

I dug my knuckles into the kitchen table, thinking, "He looks like an animal. A fat, squishy animal with little eyes, and zits all over his face, and hair that always looks dirty no matter how often it's washed." And all the time he kept looking at me with those little close-together eyes, and his mouth open, and his tongue hanging out, and the drool. The never-ending, god-awful drool. "Oh, Lord," I thought, "he's my brother and sometimes I can't stand him."

"Fredlet, please give Dorrie the clay. Come on now, like a good boy, and I'll get your blocks out." Somehow I had automatically slipped into the coaxing voice we all used for him. Then I reached for the clay.

"Mine. Mine. Fredlet's clay. Make Poor Cat like Dorrie." And then he ran, except it was more like lumbering, into the living room. I could hear him thumping around and singing in a sort-of voice, "Poor Cat, my Poor Cat. Fredlet have." It was Poor

Cat that made me run after him. I got to the door just in time to see him put the hunk of clay on the coffee table and pick up the green ceramic cat and rock it in his arms. "Poor Cat. Fredlet—Poor Cat," he chanted over and over and over.

I never knew why Fredlet called the green cat Poor Cat. And with Fredlet the things you didn't know you just had to figure on never knowing, because he couldn't explain them, even if he knew, which he didn't. Of all the things I had done in ceramics the green cat was my favorite. There had always been something special about that cat. I can still close my eyes and feel the clay, the way my fingers shaped it and smoothed it. I'll never forget the way I felt the day I lifted it out of the kiln. For once it had all worked out: the expression on the cat's face; the arch of the back; even the glaze came out the way I had seen it in my head. I guess I'd known even before Guntzie said anything. But her words were important and I stored them away in my mind somewhere to be savored over and over. "It's good, Dorrie. Really good. I always knew you had the feel. That cat has character. You just have to look at him to know that."

My mother and father really liked the cat, and ever since I gave it to them last Christmas, Mom had tried to keep it on the coffee table, and keep a special eye on Fredlet when he was around it. For some reason Fredlet was drawn to that cat, and called him Poor Cat. And loved him.

Anyhow, Fredlet rocked the cat back and forth. And I held my breath. "Guess what, Fredlet," I said, "I'm going to make you your very own cat. The green cat is tired now and wants to go to bed. Give it to Dorrie like a good boy." Fredlet lunged toward the sofa and dropped the cat onto the cushion. "Poor Cat tired. Dorrie make Fredlet cat."

Back in the kitchen, I broke off two pieces of clay, rolled them into balls, and stuck them together. I pinched two ears on top and gave it to Fredlet. "Okay, Fredlet. Here's your nice cat. Now sit down and play with it and let me get my work done." Fredlet plopped down on the kitchen floor and started to stroke the cat till pretty soon it looked like a gray lump—all blah and wet.

I remember in ceramics class when Guntzie said, "Wedging clay is a great way to get rid of your hostilities. A lot better than breaking dishes. And it's good for the clay too. Gets the air bubbles out."

And I really went after that clay with a vengeance, throwing one piece on the board as hard as I could, then throwing the other piece on top of it, then dividing it in two and starting over. It made a sort of "thwacking" sound. And with every thwack I thought, "There, that's Fredlet," or "That's for Mom, here's one for Dad." I sometimes wondered if anybody had as many hostilities as I did. Or as many questions. Like why? Why do my parents have a son with an IQ of about one-fifth of theirs? And why was Fredlet home when he could be away somewhere, in a home or something?—except knowing my mother and father I knew he never would be. Or why when they have a perfectly good daughter do they talk about Fredlet, Fredlet, Fredlet till I could scream? I'm not exactly a gorgon to look at: tall, but not too, brown hair that really is brown and not mousey, and what my grandmother says are good bones. But I'm not Fredlet.

After a while the wedging got to be mechanical. Cut and throw, cut and throw. And off in the corner Fredlet sat patting the blob and crooning, "Poor Cat. Fredlet have Poor Cat." The clay was wet and slimy by then, and my stomach almost turned inside out when he snuffled loudly, wiped his nose on his hand, and kept right on petting that revolting cat. "My God, it's no wonder I'm hostile, with that for a brother." Fredlet was eleven—and a really big eleven—but he had a little mind. From the back he looked like he should play football; from the front you knew why he played blocks. My stomach lurched again and I tried to swallow the bitter taste of guilt.

Wrapping the clay in plastic, I cleaned up the board. "Come on, Fredlet. Dorrie has to go to the store for paper. Let's get cleaned up." "No. Fredlet stay with Poor Cat," he said, rolling the glob of clay up and down his face and licking it with his too-big tongue.

"Fredlet want candy? Come on, Fredlet. Let's get candy," I said, picking up his clay cat with a paper towel as Fredlet scrambled to his feet. "Candy man, candy man. Fredlet want candy," he shouted. I could have kicked myself for bribing him. It was one of the big gripes I had with my mother. I kept telling her he had to learn sometime. Except he didn't.

I got him over to the kitchen sink and tried not to throw up as I took wet paper towels to get the crud off his face. Anyhow, we finally got out of the apartment, and down in the self-service elevator. Fredlet didn't like the elevator much except to try and push all the buttons at once. He mostly just hung on to the rail in back and howled all the way down.

Once outside, I stood on the apartment house steps for a while and looked up and down Madison Avenue. I guess I think New York in spring is about the greatest thing there is. Even with pollution, and hardly a tree in sight.

Somehow we got across Madison Avenue at Ninetieth Street and made it to the stationery store and out again with paper for me and a box of sour balls for Fredlet. Now, the really dumb thing on my part was letting him carry his own candy. We were halfway across Madison Avenue when Fredlet let out a piercing scream and threw his hands up over his ears. Sour balls rolled every which way. There he stood right in the middle of the street making this ungodly noise, with his eyes scrunched closed and his hands over his ears. I'd often thought that Fredlet had dog ears. You know, the kind that hear things no one else ever does. Then way off in the distance I heard a siren. "It's okay, Fredlet. It's just a noise and it's not even near us. Come on."

The light changed, horns blew, and Fredlet stood still. I grabbed his arm and tried to push him across the street. My face felt as though it were on fire, and I pretended not to hear the cab driver who kept shouting, "Okay, girlie, get that kid outta the street."

"Open your eyes, please, Fredlet. Nothing's going to hurt you, I promise." It seemed like hours before he let me push him the rest of the way across the street. Once we were inside our apartment house, Fredlet broke away and started up the stairs.

I stood for a few minutes in the deserted hall. I could hear the sound of the stereo coming from Guntzie's studio, so I knew she hadn't gone to the dinner-dance after all. I'd had the feeling she wasn't going to make it. Guntzie must have turned up the volume just then because the music filled the hall— Aaron Copland's *Appalachian Spring*—that really neat part, "Simple Gifts." And suddenly I knew that Guntzie was celebrating her gift to herself—not having to go to the Parents' Club Dinner-Dance in that grungy old black crepe dress. I could almost see her in her cluttered apartment that was filled with the smell of linseed oil and turpentine, and Guntzie feeling absolutely pastoral—and free.

For a minute I was really tempted to go in—to get

away from Fredlet for a minute—but by that time he was all the way to the fourth floor and leaning over the railing making echo noises, and had even forgotten about his ears hurting—for the moment at least. And then all hell broke loose.

My parents were home. They couldn't possibly have been home yet. But they were. They must have only stayed for the celery and olives.

"Dorrie? Where are you?" called my father, and I took off up the stairs two at a time. I knew I'd hear it about letting Fredlet go up the stairs instead of the elevator.

Fredlet has this heart thing—a defect of some kind that he was born with. I don't really understand it because I'm pretty awful where anything to do with medicine is concerned. I could never be a nurse. Never. But anyway, he has it and there's nothing much anybody can do about it except watch him a lot. And not let him overdo, like running up three flights of steps.

By the time I got to the fourth floor my father was standing by the open apartment door and Fredlet had collapsed in a heap on the floor holding his hands over his ears. "Oooh, noise, oooh. Hurt ears."

"Dorrie," said Dad, "what's wrong with Fred?"

"Oh, for Pete's sake," I answered, "he heard the sirens is all."

Just then Mom came running down the hall. She looked nice—her hair had been recently frosted and she was getting used to her contacts—but she had that flustered look she got when Fredlet was involved. "Dorrie, what's the matter with Fred? You didn't let him walk up all those stairs, did you? Look how blue his lips are. Oh, Joe, I knew we shouldn't have gone. It's good we didn't stay any longer." And suddenly she looked as if a light had gone out inside of her. And even her perfume smelled stale.

I climbed over Fredlet, who sounded like a stuck pig by that time. "Yes, he came up the stairs. And no, I didn't let him. He heard the sirens again, and they weren't even close by."

"Oh, poor Fred," said my mother. "I think it really does hurt his ears, Dorrie. I'll see if I can quiet him down." She bent over and stroked his sweated-back hair. "Poor Fred. Come along, let's get to bed."

Poor Fredlet, poor Fredlet, poor Fredlet. I wanted to scream.

"Thanks for sitting. It was a big help. How was he, anyhow?" My father put his arm around my shoulders. Maybe if he hadn't I never would have said it.

Suddenly it was as if a hundred firecrackers exploded in my head. I could see Fredlet slobbering into that awful clay. I could hear the cab driver's yell. I saw sour balls rolling all over Madison Avenue.

"He was like he always is. An *animal*, that's what." And I ran into my room and slammed the door.

Standing at my window, I tried to breathe in all of that spring night. I rested my head on the metal grating that had been put on all the apartment windows to protect Fredlet. The metal was cool on my forehead. "Oh, God, Fredlet's the animal, and I'm in the cage."

4

When I first woke up I wallowed in the Saturday morningness of it all. I stretched my legs all the way out till my toes touched the spools at the end of my bed and reached my arms up over my head till my hands caught hold of the headboard. The sunlight and the window grating formed a kind of extended tic-tac-toe game on the opposite wall, and in my head I was already splashing giant red *x*'s and *o*'s all over the wall. Until I remembered.

Echoes of the night before bounced around my mind, and I stuffed my face in the pillow trying to cool away the hot shame that poured over me.

"An animal. He's nothing but an animal."

I guess I knew I had to get up and say something to my father. I mean you just don't go around calling your brother an animal and then act like you hadn't. At least not when your brother's like mine. I think I was finding out that one of the problems of letting it all hang out was that sometimes you had to stuff it all back in. And you can't. Like trying to put all those stack-up potato chips back in the can after they've been in a bowl.

Well, I dragged myself up, fiddled around making my bed, brushing my hair, anything to kill time. Dad was at the breakfast table reading the paper. I watched him for a few minutes, studying his face. The lines and furrows looked new and unfamiliar. His hairline was receding and at the edges his hair was gray. It couldn't have just happened, but I didn't remember ever noticing it before—my father was going gray.

"Hi, Dad. Uh, about last night, you know, what I said and all . . . I'm . . ."

"Morning, Dorrie," he said, hardly looking at me. "Forget about last night. We all say things we don't mean. It's hard on all of us at times."

He took up another section of the paper, then put it down and looked at me. "This business with Fred —any child like him, I mean—it's like a load that never gets any lighter. But it's worse for your mother. You and I can, oh, have other things." Dad's voice was swallowed up into the coffee cup, and then he folded a piece of newspaper and propped it up in front of him.

I stared out of the kitchen window at the wall of the next apartment house. For a minute I'd thought he was really going to say something, that we could have a conversation where I could tell Dad how I sometimes felt about Fredlet, and he would tell me why I felt that way. And afterward he would pat me on the head and make everything all right, the way he used to when I was little and skinned my knee.

But it didn't work that way. Dad kept reading and I kept staring at that blasted wall, and tying knots in my bathrobe belt.

"But I did mean it," I thought. "Why can't he see that I really did mean it. Last night, at least."

I shook some cornflakes into a bowl and pulled my chair up to the table, concentrating on the back of the cereal box. Dad stood up.

"I've got to run now, Dorrie. I have a brief to get ready."

"Where are you going?" asked my mother, coming into the kitchen. "Did you forget we have to take Fred to the dentist?"

"Oh, good lord, is that today? I've got to get to the office. This brief is due Monday."

"But you promised. You know what Fred's like at the dentist. I purposely made the appointment for a Saturday because you said you'd come with us."

"I'm sorry, Elizabeth. I really am. But I have a full day's work. That court case last week ran over and I'm a day behind."

"Never mind," said Mom, pouring herself a cup of coffee. But her tone of voice said much more. Like:

"I'll manage, but it won't be easy—"

"After all, you said you'd help—"

"You could go to the office this afternoon—"

"Or tomorrow."

"I'm sure you can manage," said Dad. "It's just for a checkup. I'm going to run now. I'll be in the office if you need me."

Mom sighed. "I guess we'll manage," she said as she left the room. She didn't stomp, but I had the feeling if Mom had been a stomper she would have stomped that morning—or slammed, or yelled. Mom was a teeth-clencher instead.

"Uh, Dorrie," said Dad from the kitchen door, "how about it? Want to do me a favor?"

"Okay. I guess so. What is it?" But I knew, without really having to ask. Fredlet, again—and again and again.

"How about going along with your mother? You know how Fred is about dentists. You'll be home by noon."

"Sure. Okay. It's okay." To me my words sounded dull and heavy.

"That's great. I'll tell your mother. Fred is sometimes a lot for her to handle alone. Thanks."

I sat in the empty kitchen looking down at the bowl of soggy cornflakes. It wasn't exactly that I minded so much having to go with Mom and Fredlet. It was more that nobody especially cared whether or not I had anything else to do. I mean, anything to do as me—Dorrie Shafer—like a drawing that just had to be done or a hunk of clay I was just aching to get my fingers around. "What are *you* doing today, Dorrie? What do you think about? What do you feel?" Instead of fredletfredletfredlet-fredletfredletfredletfredletfredlet.

Fredlet shuffled into the kitchen. He was carrying that blasted Sears, Roebuck catalog and his face looked round and blank.

"How do, Dorrie. How do." He put the catalog on the chair and sat on it. Maybe he liked the feeling of knowing where it was, because when he wasn't "reading" it he sat on it.

He dumped Cheerios into his bowl and poured the milk my mother always measured out into his pitcher on his cereal. He started shoveling the cereal in. That's something we had to watch a lot, otherwise he'd just eat and eat and eat—and he was already chunkier than he should be.

"Hey, Fredlet," I said. "We're going out. Let's get ready to go."

"Go bus? Vrrmm, vrrmm. Fredlet go bus."

I often thought that if Fredlet hadn't been born the way he was, maybe he'd rather have been a bus driver than anything in the world. I'm not sure, though. Maybe if he hadn't been retarded, he wouldn't have wanted to be a bus driver anymore. I mean, he would have been smart enough to know about traffic, and muggers, and smart-alec kids. It's sad, kind of.

We could have taken a taxi. That would have been so simple. Two empty cabs even slowed down to see if we were interested, but all the time Fredlet kept saying, "Bus—go bus. Fredlet go vrrmm." So we waited for the bus.

While my mother paid the fare I settled Fredlet on the long seat behind the driver. And right away he started turning his imaginary steering wheel.

"Vrrmm, vrrmm, vrrmm," he roared as the bus bounced down Lexington Avenue. "Vrrmm, vrrmm." He twisted that wheel right and left. "Vrrmm, screeeech, whoa," he shouted every time the bus slowed down.

Farther back by the center door there was a bunch of boys hooting and calling out, "That's right, kid. You get us there. Vrrmm, vrrmm." My face burned. I looked over at my mother, but she was staring out the windows on the other side. Staring out as hard as she could.

All of a sudden something bounced off Fredlet's head and rolled down the front of him. "Come along, Fred. We're almost ready to get off," said Mom, tugging at his sleeve, but Fredlet shook her off and bent down to get the scrunched-up paper cup. For a minute he held it gently in his hand as if it were—oh, I don't know—maybe a butterfly. Then he grabbed my hand and pulled me back toward the laughing boys.

"Here—here—here's your paper and how-do-you-do-today," said Fredlet, bowing to the boys. He put his hand out to the biggest boy and said, "How do *you* do today?" and the way he said it you just knew that Fredlet wanted to know. Really. The boy looked funny, then he looked at his friends, then he blushed. Then he shook Fredlet's hand.

"Come on, Fredlet. We're going to miss our stop." I got him off that bus, somehow. And for a moment I thought maybe I was going to cry—right there in the middle of Lexington Avenue.

"Oh, Mom," I said, "he talks to everyone. Someday he's going to get hurt."

My mother caught hold of Fredlet's arm. "He's friendly. Don't take that away from him. When I walk him to school every day there are people all along the way who speak to him, and know him by name."

All of a sudden it occurred to me that I'd never thought very much about what Mom and Fredlet did all day. I knew Fredlet went to a special school in a converted brownstone on Eighty-third Street. I'd even been there for programs and all. But I never thought about it being an everyday thing.

Fredlet really didn't seem to care where we were going till we opened the door of Dr. Jason's waiting room. I guess it was the smell that told him. "Oooh —oooh—oooh," he moaned, clapping his hand on his jaw. "Oooh—oooh," and he shuffled across the waiting room and curled up in a large chair. He put his head down under his arm like some giant wailing bird.

I sat as far away from him as I could and hid my face behind a *Time* magazine. "Maybe nobody will know I'm with him," I hoped, trying to tune out his moaning. Wouldn't you know it, but some old busybody started in. "Oh, the poor thing. Does he have a toothache?" My mother answered her, but I wouldn't have bothered.

"No, not really. It's time for a checkup and he doesn't like dentists much. But Dr. Jason's very good with him."

"Oh, the poor thing," the old hag babbled on. "How old is he?"

I clutched the magazine as hard as I could. "Oh, why doesn't she shut up?" I thought. "He's not a little thing, and it's none of her business how old he is. Oh, why does Mom even talk to her?"

Just then the nurse spoke to my mother. "Mrs. Shafer, we're ready for Fred now." Mom got this what-do-we-do-now look on her face. "Come on, Dorrie. Let's see if we can get him to go in," she said to me in a voice that said point-blank, "You know we can't." Mom stood beside Fredlet. "Come along, Fred. It's your turn now. Let's go see Dr. Jason." Fredlet never stopped his wailing. He never took his head out from under his arm. "Please, Fred, show Dorrie what a good boy you are. When you're all finished, we'll have ice cream."

"You try," she said, stepping back. Suddenly I felt as if a hundred eyes were boring into my back. I tried to pull Fredlet's arm away from his head, but he just burrowed deeper into the chair.

"Fredlet. Please, Fredlet. For me, Dorrie."

Just then Dr. Jason came up behind me. "Need any help here?" he asked. As soon as Fredlet heard his voice he shut up. "Okay, Fred. Let's go," said Dr. Jason, taking hold of Fredlet's arm. "Come along. I have a lot to show you in my office, and I want to clean those teeth."

Fredlet stumbled to his feet. His face was streaked with real tears, and for some reason I was surprised. Dr. Jason swooped Fredlet away and waved Mom and me back onto the couch all in one gesture.

I buried my face back in *Time* magazine, hoping my mother wouldn't talk to me. But she did. "It's funny, but he's always better for someone else." I bit my lip to keep from saying what I thought. "You're his mother. You ought to be able to handle him." I read the same words over and over.

"Aaw—help—Maa." All of a sudden the god-awful screams tore through the office. I could feel my mother stiffening on the couch next to me, but I wouldn't look at her. "Aaach—no—no."

The nurse stuck her nose out into the waiting room. "Don't worry, Mrs. Shafer. The doctor's really not hurting him at all."

"Oh, I'm sure he's not, but shouldn't I go back there with him?"

"Oh, no," hurried the nurse. "We can manage Fred better alone, I think." And she pulled her head back into the office, this time closing the door.

The chokes and screams reached through that closed door like giant fingers closing around me.

And in the background I kept hearing my mother's inane conversation with that stupid woman. "Oh, I'm sure he's all right. It's just hard for him to understand."

All of a sudden I felt encased in ice. I wasn't sure whether my feet or hands would move. My throat felt frozen. I knew I had to get out of that waiting room. I couldn't stand it another minute.

And I ran. I threw the magazine on the table and I ran. The elevator door was just closing as I pushed my way in. Huddled against the back wall, I tried to will my legs to stop shaking. My ears strained to hear Fredlet's screams. I only heard the hum of the elevator.

Without thinking, I headed toward Fifth Avenue, then headed north—past St. Patrick's, past Tiffany's, past Schwarz's. I half ran, half walked, as if something were chasing me. Almost without thinking I was back on Madison Avenue. Digging change out of my pocket, I ran for a bus and collapsed into a seat. "I've got to go somewhere," I thought. "But not home. No place that has anything to do with Mom or Fredlet."

I got off at Eighty-eighth Street, but I didn't want to go home. I don't remember how, but I found myself, as if suddenly awake, standing on Fifth Avenue in front of the Guggenheim Museum. When you grow up in New York you get to go to a lot of places, like the Planetarium, or Rockefeller Center, or the Metropolitan Museum, without thinking much about them. They're just there. But for me the Guggenheim had always been a special place. Maybe because I'd grown up only three blocks away and used to roller-skate up and down Fifth Avenue. I can still remember trying to get my roller skate swirls on the sidewalk to look like the concrete spiral of the building.

I never will forget the first time I went inside, on a grade school field trip. I felt it even then, something of the color and intensity that washed over me. And I argued with the other kids who wanted to go back to the Metropolitan and see the mummies for the seventy millionth time.

Ever since that day I'd gone back every chance I'd gotten. And it was always the same, and always different. That day, as always, I took the elevator to the top floor. As I started down the gently sloping ramp I could feel myself unwind. The colors seemed to shout and whisper at once, all around me. And I was part of it all.

5

As I wound my way to the lower part of the ramp I saw Guntzie standing in front of Kandinsky's *Several Circles*. For a few minutes I hung back and watched Guntzie studying the picture. That was an electric experience in itself. I once saw a cat watching a dragonfly on the other side of a screen door—and that cat watched that dragonfly with every inch of its catness.

And that was how Guntzie studied a painting. With every inch of her being. The really great thing about it was that Guntzie looked at everything that way, even the things we did in art class at Miss Benson's—things that a lot of times were blah, or tried to say too much. But Guntzie usually managed to dredge something out of them. Something that maybe we hadn't always known was there.

Guntzie was small and wiry, with closely cropped gray curls—but it wasn't the kind of gray that said old. Just as I couldn't think of Guntzie as being old, I couldn't think of her as ever having been young, either. The kind of young that chewed bubble gum or jumped rope or had a doll's house. That day, as usual, she was dressed in corduroy pants and a windbreaker. I guess Guntzie was what you'd call a stark individualist. Somehow I think she was doing her own thing long before it was the thing to do.

Guntzie managed to stay herself, even at Miss Benson's where everybody seemed to end up like everybody else. I guess if you're good enough you can do that. I wondered if I'd ever be that good.

She put her hand up to get a change of perspective. I moved up next to her and said, "It's just circles, isn't it? But it's a lot more, too. It makes me feel—oh, I don't know—like there's something there."

"That's it, Dorrie," said Guntzie, swinging around. "That's what makes it so good. Because it says something to you and to me—but not the same thing."

"It says to me that I'd like to be in one of them— the circles, I mean—kind of drifting into space. Maybe into another dimension."

Guntzie looked at the painting and laughed. "Hmmm, I wonder where you'd end up. Would you take someone with you or go alone?" It was an old game Guntzie and I used to play when I was little and she took me to museums. We were always trying to figure out what was in the cup the man in the painting was holding, or whether the little boy in the ruffled collar had a stiff neck, or if there was a worm in the still-life apple. Guntzie always said, "Look beyond the paint. Get inside and feel—feel—feel." But that particular Saturday I wasn't playing the game. And suddenly Guntzie knew it.

"Come on, let's go. I think we've both had enough for today. Anyway, I left the windows open in the studio and that place can't take too much fresh air."

Neither of us said anything until we got to the apartment door and Guntzie said, "Come on in and we'll have a cup of tea. It's never too warm for tea." I smiled to myself, remembering hot summer days—days when the heat seemed to bounce from one building to the next—when Guntzie had gone right on brewing her tea. And never anything as prosaic as ordinary tea bags, but always leaves from cans with exotic pictures. And always drunk from dime-store mugs with broken handles.

If I hadn't known that Guntzie's apartment was in the same building as ours I would have thought that I, like Alice, had fallen down a rabbit hole into another world. It was a world of color and smell and touch.

In the middle of the living room, or what should have been the living room, was an absolutely huge wooden work table with different-colored paint dribbles hardened on it. Ridges of blue and yellow were smeared over with blobs of red and green. The walls of the room were off-white and were usually covered with pictures that varied with the season, with Guntzie's mood, or what she had or hadn't sold recently.

On the wall by the door hung the dulcimer. It was almost three feet long and made of spruce wood. I remember the months Guntzie had spent making it: the just-so measurements, the careful cutting and sanding and staining. I'll always remember her sitting on the floor polishing and repolishing it with an old rag of an undershirt she'd gotten from the super. And all the while humming a faraway song. Off-key.

The potter's wheel stood in one corner next to the kiln, and in front of the almost-to-the-ceiling windows were two easels and two stools. Guntzie dropped her jacket on the table, went to the window, and started fiddling with the shade until the light was just right. Then she pulled out the easel and turned it slightly.

"Okay, what do you think? And don't you dare say 'I think it's nice' without looking at it."

And then she lit a cigarette and sat on the edge of the table. In a minute she was down off the table and walking around the room. That was the thing about Guntzie. She was really, really good, but with every painting it was as though she was never really sure. I remember her saying, "Everything you do is a new beginning. Don't ever take anything for granted."

It always made me feel funny when Guntzie asked me what I thought of her work. Me? What could I say? I usually liked everything she did, but Guntzie wouldn't let you off with just that. I'd found out, though, that sometimes if I kept quiet long enough she answered her own questions. The painting on the easel was an abstract of the old carousel in Central Park. I knew that because she had told me when she started working on it. There was lots of color—red and gold, and almost black green. But it could have been any carousel anywhere—with a bit of the feeling you get on a Ferris wheel in it too. I really did like it. Just as I started to open my mouth, Guntzie went over and turned the easel another couple of inches. "I've been 'living with' this to see if it's right. I think it is," she said as she let the window shade snap all the way to the top. "Now let's have some tea. You close the windows, please."

As I closed the row of windows I knew that it would take more than one afternoon's worth of fresh air to get the smells out of the studio. I breathed deeply, sorting them in my head: the damp, musty smell of the clay; the rich smell of oils; the baked heat of the kiln.

I went over and flopped in an orange beanbag chair and surveyed the clutter of the studio, trying to pretend I was seeing it for the first time. But it was hard to do. Too much of my life was wound up in this room. Everything meant something to me. The wheel was where I'd thrown my first pot. The kiln was the one I'd used to fire my first bowl, and a clay mold of my five-year-old hand that Guntzie had helped me glaze blue with red fingernails. I'd sat on those stools by the window long before my feet reached to the ground. Even the corner of the room where I was sitting, with the beanbag chairs and the bentwood rocker, and the straw mats rolled up on the floor, and the books, meant something. When I was little I'd called it the talking corner. I'd had a lot of conversations there: some about art, or me, or Mom and Dad and me, or Mom and Dad and Fredlet and me.

"I guess what I like about this place is that it's so essential. Everything here's so important. It's so basic, sort of."

"Yes, it is basic, I'll say that," said Guntzie as she handed me a cup of tea and settled herself Indian-style on the floor. In my mind I was busy comparing Guntzie's apartment with ours upstairs. My mother was big on polished furniture and dust ruffles.

I was startled when Guntzie said, "Okay, is it anything you want to talk about?"

"What do you mean?" I asked.

"Whatever it is that makes you want to go floating off into space."

I climbed out of the beanbag chair—that's the only way to get out of one—and went over and took a piece of clay out of the crock. I talk better with clay in my hands. I guess it's sort of like a cigarette with some people.

"Oh, it's nothing, I guess. Just me acting rotten

again. You don't know how many resolutions I make."

"Anything special happen to set you off?" asked Guntzie.

"Hah! When? Last night or today?"

"Well, for starters, last night."

"Oh, nothing. Last night I just told my father his son was an animal is all."

"What about today?" One thing I have to say about Guntzie: she doesn't look all horrified and shocked no matter what you tell her. She doesn't seem to feel she has to say, "Oh, no," the way my mother does, so I'll know how straight she is. I mean, I *know* how straight my mother is.

Guntzie interwove her fingers and bent them back. I guess if there was only one feature you could notice about Guntzie, it would have to be her hands. They remind me of apple trees—strong and gnarled. The knuckles are large and her fingers short, almost stubby, with the nails filed straight across. And they are never still. It's almost as if Guntzie's hands are always reaching for something—a brush or a pencil or a piece of clay. The only time Guntzie's hands are really quiet is when she's working.

"All right, last night you called your brother an animal," and Guntzie let that word just hang there, and the way it hung—over the silence of the studio— was a hundred times worse than anything she could have said.

"What did you do today?"

And all of a sudden I didn't want to tell her. But I knew I would. I'd have to. There's something about Guntzie's eyes—like birds' eyes, all sharp and darting—that always makes me start talking.

"Oh, today was beautiful. I went to help my mother take Fredlet to the dentist and I ran out and left them there. I got up out of that waiting room and left. Just left."

"Why?"

Guntzie's word sounded like a shot. She got up and went over to the cabinet under the window and came back with a stack of prints and started sorting them. But still, that "why" was waiting for me.

"Why? I don't know why. Yes I do. Because he was howling like an animal and I didn't know what to do. And I'm, I'm—oh, I don't know."

I squashed the lump of clay as hard as I could and began rolling it into a coil.

"Have you selected a print for your acrylic painting yet?"

I looked at Guntzie as if I really hadn't heard her. "Have I done what?"

"Have you gotten your canvas ready yet?" Guntzie jumped up and put the prints into the file cabinet, then gathered up the mugs.

"What's that got to do with anything?" I asked, shaping the clay into a ball again.

"It has everything to do with it, Dorrie." Guntzie put the cups in the sink and went to sit in front of the easel with the carousel on it. "Fredlet's not going to get much smarter." Guntzie was one of the few people who ever talked right out about how smart Fredlet was, or rather, how smart Fredlet wasn't. "And plenty of times you're going to think he's repulsive."

"But he is repulsive. Sometimes I can't stand him, or Mom or Dad either."

"Or yourself?"

"Yes, or me either. And I can't wait till college, or after, to be really free."

"Sometimes freedom isn't all that free. Anyway, what have you done that's constructive?"

I was beginning to wish I'd stayed at the dentist's, or never gone to the Guggenheim, or never come in for a cup of tea.

"Look, Dorrie," said Guntzie, taking the canvas off the easel and leaning it against the wall, "I don't mean to be hard on you." She stopped for a minute. "Well, maybe I do—because you're wasting time. Fredlet's not going to change, so why wear yourself out fighting it. But for heaven's sake do something. Start on your painting. Make a pot. Do some sketches. But do something."

"But I did. I wedged clay last night and I . . ."

"You wedged clay. Wonderful. Okay, now what are you going to do with it? Do you know the last important thing you did was that green cat, and that was before Christmas."

"Poor Cat. That's what Fredlet calls it."

"I know. I've heard him. He must see something in it."

"What could he see?" I asked, still feeling the sting of Guntzie's words.

"I don't know. We'll never know, but he sees something. Something only for Fredlet. The way we were talking at the museum about the Kandinsky. Something for everyone who wants to look. Even Fredlet. Oh, and speaking of the cat, this year we're including ceramics in the Spring Festival. Come look at the outline I've made for where to put what in the art show. I'm counting on you and some of the others to help me set up."

Guntzie took the list down from the wall and handed it to me. "Ann and Pat will help, I'm sure."

Spring Festival was really *the* thing at Miss Benson's, with a concert and an art show and all the classrooms open. Judging by the junk hanging up in the classrooms you'd think no one ever got below a 95 at Miss Benson's—and that's a lot of stuff. But the concert and the art show were really important. It seems as though we started getting ready in September. Especially in art. Or maybe I just cared more about art. The rest was trimming, but maybe that's what the parents paid all the tuition for—the trimmings.

I got this clammy feeling every time I thought of the art show. It was the kind of thing I tried not to think about—but did, all the time. Last year I'd won second place even though I was just a freshman. But this year—just maybe . . . I held the thought the way I used to hold a handful of soapsuds when I was little, as if the slightest movement might make them vanish. And if I won first prize (my insides shuddered for having actually thought it), what would my parents say? "Dorrie—Dorrie—Dorrie—Dorrie, our daughter. Look what she's done." I shivered, and my soapsuds thoughts disappeared.

I stuck the list back on the wall. "I've got to go. Tonight is that mixer at school—yech. I don't know why I let Ann and Pat talk me into it."

Guntzie added some water to the clay being reclaimed. "Oh, and Dorrie, be sure and bring the ceramic cat back in so we can include it in the show. I still think it's the best thing you've done."

The words came out in spite of myself. "Well, I better bring it in right away then. With Fredlet around it won't last long."

6

I get lost pretty easily. I
don't mean getting on the wrong subway or heading
west when I mean east, but the nice kind of lost—in
a book or a picture. I've been a lot of places that
way. I've been to Narnia and Wonderland and
Tara. And that particular night of the day I left
Fredlet at the dentist I was at Manderley. I could
feel the rain on my cheeks and sense the presence of
the great stone house behind me and the Cornish
coast before me. It came as a shock when my bed-
side light blinked and I looked up just in time to see
lightning streak the sky outside. I shook my head,
feeling as though I were coming back from a great
distance. The clock next to the bed said one-thirty.
I turned it to face the wall.

I was just getting back into *Rebecca* when
there was a knock on my bedroom door and my father stuck his head into the room. "Everything all

right, Dorrie? I saw your light on as I went to lock up."

"Sure, Dad. Fine. I just got lost in this book is all. How come you're still up?"

"Well, it's not exactly that I've been up," said Dad sitting on the foot of my bed. "I stayed up to watch a movie but must have fallen asleep. How was the mixer?"

I made a face. "Awful. I'm never going to another one. It was really queer. Tons of freshman were there, and the band stunk, and the chaperones kept patrolling the whole place like they thought we were a bunch of convicts or something."

"Was everything all right? I mean, there wasn't any trouble, was there?"

Sometimes I don't understand parents. I'm not sure they'd really want to know if there was trouble, and I'm not sure I'd tell them. "Trouble? How could there be trouble? The place was crawling with rent-a-cops and teachers and parents. For Pete's sake, they even followed you into the bathroom. It might have been more fun if there had been trouble."

"That's quite a storm out there," said Dad, so I knew right away that he hadn't really cared about the mixer at all. "How did you and your mother make out taking Fred to the dentist?"

I gave Dad a kind of funny look. "Uh, Dad, uh, what did Mom say, about the dentist, I mean?"

"Well, to tell you the truth, Dorrie, I forgot to

ask her. But Fred seemed fine tonight so I guess everything was all right."

"Not exactly. I mean, I guess Fredlet was all right. But are you sure Mom didn't say anything?"

"About what, Dorrie? What are you getting at?" Dad's voice sounded impatient.

"It was me—I left. Fredlet was screaming and yelling—that was after he moaned all over the waiting room, and all of a sudden I just couldn't stand it. And I left."

"You left? You left?" Dad kept saying, like he heard me but he didn't know what I was saying. "You left? What do you mean you left?"

"Oh, Dad, I couldn't stand it. All of a sudden . . . you know . . . the way people stare at him and ask questions, and then the noise. I just had to get out, and I did."

I watched my father's face. It seemed like ages before he said anything. I could hear the rain slapping on the window, and watched the curtains getting wet without doing anything about it. "But, Dad," I said, "I just couldn't stand it anymore." Still my father didn't say a word. "I know it was rotten and irresponsible and everything. I know what you must be thinking of me." Somehow I felt as though I had to keep on talking. If only Dad had reacted. If only he'd yelled, or told me to grow up, or something. "I don't know why I act this way. Why do I?"

When Dad finally spoke, it was as if we had been

having two parallel conversations. They never met. "It's your mother I'm worried about, Dorrie. I don't see how she can manage much longer."

It was like being in a fun house. I was talking and not getting through to Dad, and then all of a sudden there he was talking about my mother.

"Mom? What do you mean about Mom?"

"Taking care of Fred," answered my father. "It's a pretty big job and she doesn't have much help. And I'm afraid that heart problem is going to give him more trouble the older he gets."

"But, Dad, Fredlet's Fredlet—same as always—and so's Mom—"

Dad tugged on his ear. "I don't know. It's beginning to wear on your mother, I'm afraid." I wasn't sure what he meant, but I thought I was supposed to say something. "Well, I'll help her. Really I will."

"I'm afraid that's not all of the answer. In another couple of years you'll be away at college, then working, and maybe even married. I guess it's partly living here that's the problem."

"But we've always lived in this apartment. What's the matter with it?"

"No—no, it's not the apartment," said Dad. "It's New York. The whole setup, our whole way of life."

My voice felt as though it had gotten away from me. "What do you mean, 'New York'? What's that got to do with anything?"

Dad went over and looked out the window, and for the first time I had the feeling that this was a real conversation, that he was really telling me something. And I think I knew deep down that this was why he had waited up, and not to see a late movie. When he spoke his voice sounded faraway. "Well, for one thing there's no family here, no one to give your mother a breather. And it's really not too safe. There's no place Fred can go out and play alone, like a backyard or something."

"But, we've got to live in New York. We just have to. Don't we?" As soon as I said it I wanted to swallow back that last question.

"That's just it. Before, it would have been hard to give up my practice without some kind of security. But now something's come up that changes all that. And aside from my work, there's no real reason why we have to live in New York."

"But we just have to. Well, for one thing there's your work. You work here." It was a stupid thing to say. I mean, he had just said something had come up about work, but for a moment I really felt like I'd found the clincher, but Dad brushed it aside like a pesky June bug.

"Dorrie, that's what I've been trying to tell you. Something's come up—a good opportunity to practice law in Maryland with ..."

"Maryland," I shrieked. "Maryland? Then you have been planning something? You really mean it?

You're not just talking? But there's nothing in Maryland. Nothing."

"Now, calm down. Nothing's settled, but your uncle Stanley's been after me to come down and practice with him ever since your grandfather died, and now his one remaining partner is going on the bench, so Stanley really needs me. And somehow, with things the way they are with Fred, this seems like a good time to make the move."

I jumped out of bed and stood facing my father. "How about the way things are with me? I have two more years of high school. It's a perfectly rotten idea and a perfectly rotten time, and there's nothing there except a dinky little town."

"Now, Dorrie, stop getting worked up and just listen. Tunbridge is not a dinky little town. In fact you've always liked it when we've visited your grandmother."

"A visit's one thing. But not to live. Never. Never. Never. I won't go. I belong in New York. I have to be here. I *have* to. It's the only place. Everything's here. What about art school? You've known forever that that's what I wanted. You promised. And what about the museums and all the galleries? There's nothing in Maryland. What do you want me to do? Raise chickens or something?"

"Dorrie Shafer, keep quiet and listen for a minute. If—and it's still a big if—if we move to Tunbridge, your mother will be near her mother and her brothers and sisters, and my sister. And they'll be able to give her a hand with Fred no matter what he needs. Think of your mother. Think of Fred."

"I'm sick of thinking of Fredlet. All we ever do is think of Fredlet."

Those words seemed to stay there in the room like smoke rings that didn't quite dissolve but just floated around overhead.

I stared at my father. His face was a study in grays, with stubbly black whiskers accenting his chin —and suddenly in a far-off corner of my mind I thought, "I'd like to paint that face."

Dad picked up a paperweight from the table and rubbed it with his thumbs. "Try and get a little perspective. We're not trying to make you unhappy, but I'm really worried about your mother. More and more. It's hard to get help in the city—and Fred's getting harder to manage. And now that I have this offer from your uncle Stanley it just seems like the time to make the move. All of a sudden living in New York just doesn't seem important."

"Important? Well, it's important to me. It's the *most important thing in the world*."

My father put down the paperweight and rubbed his forehead. "Nothing's decided. We're still in the thinking stage. Anyway, just remember you have your whole life ahead of you."

"My whole life?" It was as though my thoughts were bigger than my head. Words pounded against my throat, but I couldn't speak.

"Get some sleep. Nothing's definite." My father went out, closing the door behind him.

Sleep—hah. As if I could have slept. It was as if my whole life had fallen apart, and my father said "Sleep." As soon as I heard his bedroom door click shut I hurled *Rebecca* across the room. Then I had to go get it because I always have terrible guilt feelings if I throw a book.

I turned off the light and tried to concentrate on just hearing the rain. I kept hearing my father's words: "Our whole way of life . . . practice in Maryland . . . the help she'd have."

I flopped over on my stomach and pounded the mattress with my fists. I was angry with my father—and with my mother. I was angry at Fredlet for making me feel that way about them.

For the next few days things were so everyday that I thought maybe I'd dreamed the whole middle-of-the-night thing. Neither Dad nor Mom said anything about moving, and I shoved the thought to the back of my mind. But every once in a while it kept popping up—sort of like trying to sit on a beach ball in the water.

At school, things had gotten to that wild end-of-the-year rat race. The seniors hardly seemed part of the school anymore; and we were all caught up in elections, Spring Festival, and plans for work-study week.

I rushed into the cafeteria a few days later and pulled up to a table with Ann and Pat. The three of us have been eating lunch together since way back in grade school. Even when we were little we hardly ever fought or ganged up two-against-one the way three people sometimes do. My mother always said it was because we were all different—that we sort of fit together like a puzzle. I'm just me—the way I am. Ann is Spanish—well, from Ecuador—and is small and beautiful. At home everyone speaks Spanish and calls her Ana, but she doesn't even have a hint of an accent and is definitely Ann at school. Pat is sort of rowdy and friendly, and always on a diet. She has a funny streak in her hair and tells everybody the sun did it. Ann and I know better.

"Hurry up, Dorrie," said Ann. "You only have ten minutes to eat before we have our class meeting —and it's the last one of the year."

I swallowed the rest of my sandwich. "Hey, what's the meeting about anyway?"

"Class elections. They're today, then more stuff about work-study. You really are in another world," said Ann. "Come on, let's go."

When we got to the assembly hall the meeting had already started and Linda Ready, who had been class president when we were freshmen, and this year too, was giving a little talk. "And I want to thank you all for the cooperation you've given me these last two years. Now that I've been elected Student Council secretary I can no longer be your president. . . ." I slouched down in my seat and groaned to myself. Linda always had liked the speech-making part of being president. "And so," Linda went on, "let's now have nominations from the floor for class president for next year."

Ann raised her hand. "I nominate Dorrie Shafer," she said, in that whispery voice of hers. "I second the nomination," said someone in the back of the room. "Ann," I gasped, grabbing her arm, "are you out of your mind?"

"You're the logical person, Dorrie," whispered Pat. "You have been vice-president for two years."

"Yes, but that's different," I whispered back. "I can't be president." Being vice-president for someone like Linda Ready was a real do-nothing job. Every year I got my picture in the yearbook under "Class Officers," and that was the end of it. Linda never needed any help and never, never got sick.

Suddenly papers were being handed out. "Vote for yourself, you have to," said Pat, poking me in the ribs. Then the ballots were collected and Linda and two other girls were counting them in the back of the room.

"We have a new president," said Linda, pausing dramatically. "Our class president for next year is Dorrie Shafer."

Everybody clapped, and Pat yelled, "Speech, speech." Then Mrs. Wentworth, our moderator, stood up and said, "Girls, girls," in that funny closed-mouth voice a lot of the teachers at Miss Benson's used. "Congratulations, Dorrie. Now let's have a little order in this room. You may carry on,

Linda." And I sat there not really able to believe it. I was thinking maybe I'd dreamed the whole thing, and wondering if Ann would think I'd really flipped if I leaned over and asked her if I was really president. It was unreal. Me—Dorrie Shafer—president of the class.

Then I got a cold, empty feeling right in the middle of my stomach. I remembered what my father had said about maybe moving to Maryland. How could I tell all these people who had voted for me that I probably wouldn't even be here. Then I thought about my mother and father, and what they would say when they found out I was going to be class president next year. I wondered if that would make them stay in New York.

I doubted it.

Thoughts kept running through my head like a ticker tape. From somewhere faraway I could hear the rest of the meeting going on. Miss Nichols talking about work-study, schedule changes—voices swirled around me.

I thought about work-study and how excited I was about teaching art, and I thought about Fredlet, and some more about moving and how I could change my parents' minds. And right then, like in some crazy old cartoon, I felt as though a light bulb had gone off in my head.

Work-study. What if, instead of teaching art, I were to go work at Fredlet's school—and really let

Dad know I was interested in Fredlet and was trying to help. Maybe then . . .

The meeting ended and girls were crowding around and congratulating me. It was a good feeling, but I was almost afraid to enjoy it. I just kept thinking what if I had to come in one of these days and say, "Sorry, everybody. We won't be here next year. Find yourselves another president."

Out in the hall I pulled Ann and Pat off to a corner. "I've got to ask you something," I said, "about work-study. What do you think would happen if I changed what I signed up for?"

"Oh, sure, Dorrie. Miss Nichols would be thrilled to have you go in there at this late date and try to change anything. What's the matter with you, anyway? You got just what you wanted, teaching art in a downtown school," said Pat, stuffing some papers into her folder.

"I know, but my father's on a kick about my brother and all, and him being too much for my mother, and maybe even moving to some god-awful town somewhere."

"What's that got to do with work-study?" asked Ann.

"Well, I'm not sure exactly," I said. "But I thought maybe if I asked Miss Nichols if I could go to Bellringers—my brother's school—it might make my father think I was interested. You know, doing something to help and all that stuff."

Ann and Pat looked at each other and rolled their eyes. "Well, you could try. Personally, I'd rather be thrown into a pit of lions. But if you want to ask if you can change everything a week before work-study, go ahead. Anyway, wouldn't Miss Guntz have a fit if you didn't do something with art next week?" Pat asked.

"Oh, Guntzie'd understand. If I don't get my father off my back I won't be here next year. I'll be down in some hole in Maryland drawing corncobs."

Pat and Ann went off to math and I went to talk to Miss Nichols and then spent the rest of the afternoon dodging my friends. I'm not sure why I was avoiding them. Miss Nichols had let me change work-study, but for some reason I just didn't want to tell them. After school I headed upstairs to the library so Pat wouldn't drag me off to Schrafft's. I had the feeling that anything I ate would turn to sawdust.

I grabbed a record from the rack and headed for the farthest carrel. Hooking the earphones on my head, I flipped the switch. The record started, but the only sounds I heard were voices. Mine, sickeningly sweet and two-faced, and Miss Nichols's, full of sympathy.

"I know it's awfully late to ask, Miss Nichols. . . ."
    "A very unselfish thing, Dorrie . . ."
"If it could be arranged . . ."
    "I'll see what I can do. . . ."
"I'd like to go to Bellringers. . . ."

"To give up your chance of teaching art . . ."

"Work with the retarded . . ."

"A credit to our school . . ."

"To understand my brother . . ."

"A very lucky boy . . ."

"To help my mother . . ."

"Make your father very proud . . ."

The record stopped, and almost without thinking I wiped it off and put it in the folder and hurried down to the empty locker room. "Well, Dorrie Shafer," I thought, "you really get the prize. Apple polisher, brown-noser, call it what you want. You're it."

I gave the heavy door a shove with my shoulder. I was surprised to see that the sun was shining.

7

I guess the things people never forget are either a lot of good or a lot of bad. And I know I'll never forget my week at Bellringers. That's what it was a lot of—good and bad.

Take the bathroom, for instance. Sometimes I felt as if I spent the whole day in that bathroom on the second floor with all the pipes wrapped in plaster, and the little round sinks with rubber stoppers, and the blackish green linoleum that humped up in places. And the smell—urine and Lysol together forever in my mind and nose.

There was a sameness about the days too. Me saying the same things, like "Flush the toilet, Billy. I'm waiting to hear it." "John-Paul, you go right back in there and pull your pants up." "Sandy, what are you doing? Oh, no, not a whole roll of toilet paper."

"That's right, Billy. Put the stopper in the sink and run the water. Stop. Oh, Billy, look at the floor."

And Billy looked, and he grinned, and he swished his hands back and forth in the brimful sink while I made a grab for the paper towels and put them all over the puddle. And with one hand I tried to get Billy's hands. But it was too late. I saw the water darkening the blue sleeves of his shirt.

"Uh-uh-uh," said Billy, holding up his dripping arms. "Uh-uh-uh." "Oh, Billy," I said. "Look at your nice shirt. Let's see if I can roll the sleeves back for you." Billy's hands and wrists were already red and chapped. As soon as I knelt down in front of him, Billy threw his sopping arms around my neck and we both went over backward.

For some crazy reason I laughed. "Uh-uh-uh," said Billy, grinning widely. Then, enjoying the game, he gave me another shove and turned and ran into one of the johns. I could see his fingers holding tight to the bottom of the door. Picking myself up off the floor, I said, "Billy, right now, open this door." I tugged on the door but wasn't surprised when it didn't budge, remembering how Fredlet turned into an almost superman when he wanted to. "Billy, please," I begged. "Uh-uh-uh," said Billy. "Billy, come on." I began to feel like an absolute fool pulling on that stupid door. "Oh, God," I thought. "He's just like Fredlet, only his name's Billy." But I knew if it had been Fredlet I never would have laughed at all. "Uh-uh-uh," said Billy.

"Anything wrong, Dorrie?" I turned to see Mrs. Sherwood, the classroom teacher, in the doorway.

"It's Billy, Mrs. Sherwood. He's in there and won't come out." Mrs. Sherwood gave a sharp rap on the bathroom door followed by a quick jerk on the handle. The door swung open. Billy was kneeling on the floor, looking up at us with a silly grin on his face.

"Billy Watkins, get up right this minute," said Mrs. Sherwood. "Now go back to the classroom. March." Although Mrs. Sherwood's voice was firm, I noticed that it was kind. Billy smiled at us vacantly, then shuffled off toward the classroom.

"Don't let them get the best of you, Dorrie. You have to stay one jump ahead of these children. I'm sure you know that from being around Fred."

"But, Mrs. Sherwood," I said. "Isn't it all so pointless. I mean, doing the same thing over and over and never seeing any results."

"Oh, Dorrie," Mrs. Sherwood said, "there are results. Sometimes very, very small ones, and you have to learn to look for them. It's the children who matter."

I followed Mrs. Sherwood back to the classroom, feeling strangely inadequate. Back in the room the children had their heads down on their desks, and several were actually asleep. I heard Billy snoring gently.

Except that the desks were large, the classroom could have belonged to a nursery school. There were Mother Goose cutouts on the walls, and red-checked curtains on the long windows. The ten tables were in the center of the room, and around the walls red and blue and yellow shelves held games and puzzles. There were no textbooks or maps in the classroom, and I knew for this group none would ever be needed. I can imagine blindness by closing my eyes, or deafness, sort of, by holding my ears. But no matter how hard I try, I can't grasp Fredlet's world, or Billy's, or Mary's.

Mary had thick brown permanent-waved hair and blue-rimmed glasses that were about an inch and a half thick. After the children were awake and were working on wooden puzzles, Mrs. Sherwood brought Mary to me. "Now, Mary, I'm going to ask Miss Dorrie to take you out in the hall and let you practice your steps." Mary stuffed her fingers in her mouth and the drool ran down on her pink sweater. Over Mary's head Mrs. Sherwood spoke to me. "Mary has to practice going up and down the steps like a big girl—one foot on each step. Would you help her, please?"

Mary took her fingers out of her mouth, and put them wet and dripping into my hand. I flinched, then hoped it hadn't shown. "Sure, Mrs. Sherwood. Come along, Mary. Show me how you go down the steps." I led Mary through the passage to the stairs and tried to keep from screaming as she stopped to examine every doorknob and finger every coat hook.

At the stairway Mary grabbed the handrail with both hands and started down the steps. Thump. She put one foot down on the step and then brought the other foot down to meet it. Thump. Down with one foot and then the other. Mary grinned at me. "No, Mary, I want you to go down like a big girl. One foot on each step. Not two feet on a step." Mary stared at me and giggled. Then she reached out and gave my hand a loud, sloppy kiss.

"Come on, Mary. Let's try again." As Mary stumped her way back to the top I wiped my hand up and down on the side of my pants. Mary stood at the top of the stairs with a look on her face like it was her birthday or something.

"Okay, Mary. Let's try it this way," I said, bending down and taking hold of one of Mary's legs. "All right, now, this foot goes down to the step below." Mary moved her foot down tentatively. "Good, Mary. Now the next foot." I took Mary's other leg. "Now, Mary, we're going to put this foot all the way down to the next step."

As I tried to work Mary's rubber-band legs, she clutched the railing and swayed back and forth. "No, no, Mary. Don't put this foot on the step with the other one. Do it like a big girl." Then I pulled one leg down to the step below. "Good girl, Mary. Let's try again." Mary quickly moved her foot down to join the other one.

I rubbed the back of my neck and swung my arms back and forth. "Okay, Mary. Here we go again." By the time we worked our way to the bottom I was beginning to wonder if I'd ever be able to straighten up again. "Good, Mary. That was good," I said, trying to get a little enthusiasm into my voice. "That was good. Now let's go up and try again."

"No," said Mary in her husky voice. "No." And she sat on the floor and rubbed her legs. "No, no, no." Big tears dripped down her face. I sat down on the bottom step and looked at her. Then I looked at my watch. I couldn't believe that it had taken us fifteen minutes to struggle down one flight of stairs. "Okay, Mary. That's all. Let's go back for lunch."

Mary stumped up the stairs grinning happily as she placed two feet on every step.

I hardly ever saw Fredlet the whole time I was at Bellringers school, and the few times I did see him, either in the playroom or in the halls, he hardly paid any attention to me. It gave me a strange feeling to see Fredlet having a life other than the one at home. I'd never really thought of him doing anything else, without us.

At noon I helped Mrs. Sherwood with the lunches, and it seemed like an endless job just for a peanut-butter sandwich. I sometimes wondered what kept Mrs. Sherwood from just handing out the lunches and saying, "Eat." She could have done that in five minutes. But oh, no, we made a real production of it. Say it was Billy's day, for instance. Mrs. Sherwood would hand Billy the lunches one at a time and say, "Whose lunch is this, Billy?"

And Billy would say something like "uh-uh-uh" and point to Mary.

Then Mrs. Sherwood would say, "That's a good boy, Billy. Now give Mary her lunch." Then Billy would shuffle across the room and put the box on Mary's desk and Mrs. Sherwood would say, "Say, 'Here's your lunch, Mary,'" and Billy would say, "Uh-uh-uh" again. And the really funny part was then Mary would say in that gravelly voice of hers, "Thank you, Billy," and of course he'd say, "Uh-uh-uh."

By that time I'd be ready to climb the walls. And there were eight more lunches to go.

Then there was the milk bit. Who could open their own milk and shouldn't be helped, and who should be helped or else they spilled it. And who ate straws, and, of course, there was Elaine who had to have a plastic cup or else she squashed the whole carton while it was still full.

Eventually, about an hour later, the room was filled with the warm smell of peanut butter and tuna fish, and with the sound of slurping. I pulled a little chair up to the window and looked out, trying to block out the sounds.

"Are you all right, Dorrie?" asked Mrs. Sherwood, sitting on a little chair next to me.

"Oh, sure," I said. "Sure, I'm fine. But . . . well, how do you stand it? I mean, every day, over and over?"

"I don't know, Dorrie. I love these children, and the parents are so grateful. Not like a normal school where the parents are always wanting to know why their little dears only got a C. And remember, Dorrie, I don't go home to a retarded child every day. That does make it easier, you know."

"I guess so," I said. But I wasn't really convinced. "Did you ever teach my brother?"

"I certainly did, and Fred was a delight. But he kept things lively." Mrs. Sherwood laughed.

"A delight?" I wondered to myself. "I don't see much delightful about him. Ugh."

"Dorrie," Mrs. Sherwood went on, "I think it's great of you to come down here and help. I hear you want to learn to understand Fred better."

I jumped up and started collecting the trash, hoping the awful feeling of hypocrisy that swept over me didn't show.

That night, as I lay in the tub trying to soak away the day, I decided I'd had enough. Four days out of five wasn't bad. "I've had it. I don't want the hassle, and anyway, tomorrow's the last day. I'm not going back. And anyway, my throat does sort of hurt." I swallowed hard. I have some of my best conversations with myself in the bathtub.

Thursday night I made sure my mother saw me spray my throat and search for the aspirin. The next morning on her way to take Fredlet to school she stopped in my room. "We're leaving now," she said. "Take care of yourself, and I'll stop and tell Mrs. Sherwood you're sick. Then I'm going on downtown. Fred needs a pair of pants."

I heard Mom getting Fredlet ready to leave and I

got this really peculiar feeling. I wasn't really sick; in fact, I wasn't even a little bit sick, and I knew it, but all of a sudden I was seethingly angry with my mother for not caring that I was sick—which I wasn't. "Fredlet needs pants. Fredlet needs pants," I said out loud. "What about what Dorrie needs?" And then I was really mad at Fredlet, and by that time I was furious with myself for being mad at everybody.

As the apartment door clicked shut I settled down in the bed trying to plan the day. A whole day. It would be a good day to throw the pot I'd been wanting to do. I could almost feel the clay against my fingers, and hear the whir of the wheel.

Finally, when I couldn't get back to sleep, I got up and went and put the kettle on, but I kept looking at the clock and thinking, "Now they'll be doing their exercise, or now it's snack time." I wandered through the empty apartment. I pushed open the door to Fredlet's room and sat on the bed looking around. "It sure doesn't look like an eleven-year-old's room," I thought, looking at the stack of picture books, the plastic cars, and the teddy bear propped on the bed. Over his bed Fredlet had insisted that Dad hang the huge picture of a whale that I had drawn years ago. The whale, silver-gray and spouting blue water, stared back at me out of large black eyes. I heard the whistle of the tea kettle and dashed into the kitchen to turn it off.

I got to Bellringers a little after ten. As I waited

to catch my breath outside the classroom, I thought, "Now you've done it. Just blown a perfectly good day." Slowly I pushed the door open. The children were marching around and around the room. Mrs. Sherwood switched off the record player. "Hi, Dorrie. Feeling better? We're glad you've come. Mary needs to practice her steps."

I held out my hand. "Come on, Mary. Let's go down the steps like a big girl."

8

Mothers are impossible. Take mine, for example. I don't think she ever has any fun. She's so hung up on doing what's right and taking care of Fredlet and cleaning the house. I don't think I'll have any children or maybe even get married. I don't think there'll be time. Draw—that's what I'm going to do, and you better believe that nothing's going to get in the way. But I'm going to be spontaneous too. Most adults aren't.

It's sad in a way. Once when I was home sick, I went through some boxes in my mother's closet and they were filled with drawings and paintings that she had done. And they were good—really good. So alive. The kind of pictures that you could step into, the way Mary Poppins did with the sidewalk paintings. They made me cry. I'm not sure whether it was because they were so good or because Mom stopped doing them. There weren't any more. That's not going to happen to me.

But to get back to how mothers are impossible. Take the conversation I had with mine the morning of Spring Festival night. All of a sudden, like pass-the-salt, she said she wasn't going—coming. Because of Fredlet.

And it wasn't the first time she had pulled that either. I remembered last year when I'd been in a play and Ann and I were gypsies and had to dance to one of Liszt's *Hungarian Rhapsodies* and my mother didn't come. Now, I'm not the world's greatest dancer, but we had practiced a lot. I had seen my father from the stage, and when I got home my mother had tried to pretend she had been there and kept telling me how good I'd been. But I knew she hadn't, and she finally said, "Oh, Dorrie, I wanted to come but Fred was upset and I wasn't sure the sitter could cope. I'm sorry." But this was the art show and my own mother had to know how important it was. My most important thing in the whole world. But there she was telling me she might not make it.

I was rushing to get to school. I couldn't find matching knee socks and my face looked all lobstery from the sunlamp. I *knew* I'd look awful for the festival, and then my mother started.

"You will understand if just your father goes to-night, won't you?"

I hate it when people say 'you will understand' because then if you don't—and I didn't that day— you're the one who feels bad instead of the person who's doing whatever it is you're supposed to understand.

"Well, I don't understand," I said, marching over to the refrigerator. "If you really cared at all you'd come."

"But, Dorrie, I can't find anyone to stay with Fred tonight. You know I want to come."

"Yeah, I'll bet," I muttered under my breath.

"What did you say?" asked my mother.

"Nothing."

"You know," Mom said in a tired way, "Mrs. Moran can't come."

"I bet if it was something you wanted to do you'd find someone."

"Dorrie, stop that right this minute. I didn't break Mrs. Moran's ankle for her. Anyway, I've already told you your father's going. And I'll be thinking of you."

"Big deal," I said, slamming the refrigerator door. "Why doesn't anyone in this house start treating me like a grown-up? It's always Dorrie do this, or Dorrie don't say that."

"To be treated like a grown-up you have to act like one," said my mother, and I knew she was going to say it before she opened her mouth. Those words make me want to throw up.

"Not that old line again," I said. "And anyway, if Fredlet were in something at school you know you'd go."

"Oh, Dorrie, come on," said Mom with a don't-be-ridiculous smile, "if Fred were in a play I wouldn't need a baby-sitter for Fred, now would I? Just think about it."

She almost had me. It made sense, but I'd be darned if I'd admit it—ever. "Well, if we had relatives like anyone else, and besides we've been working for just ages on Spring Festival."

Mom poured herself another cup of coffee. "I know, Dorrie, and I'm sorry. I tell you what. I'll see how Fred is this afternoon. Maybe if he's fairly calm we can bring him. He's very good in church and he just loves to go out."

"Mother, this isn't church, for Pete's sake. We're not even talking about church. Oh, never mind, I've got to go. We're having dress rehearsal this morning. At least I managed to get the green cat to school before Fredlet did something to it."

After school, Guntzie, Pat, Ann, and I finished setting up the art show. It looked great—almost like one of those posh, small galleries downtown, except that schools always smell of chalk and sweat—and galleries don't. "It looks nice, kids," said Guntzie, standing back and shading her eyes against the late-afternoon sun. "It's a big help being able to use the larger room this year."

"Everything really does look nice, doesn't it," said Ann, picking her blazer up from the floor. "I can't believe tonight's almost here."

"Me neither," said Pat. "Hey, I've gotta go. I want to wash my hair and my mother said we're all eating at five-thirty so I can get back here in time. Let's go. You coming, Dorrie?"

I was kneeling on the floor trying to get a row of papier-mâché animals to look more "at ease" on the table. "Uh, you all go on. I want to finish here. Every time I get the elephant standing up, the giraffe falls over. See you tonight."

"Thanks, girls. Good luck tonight," called Guntzie as Pat and Ann went out. "Wait a minute, Dorrie, I have some wire and we'd better prop those creatures up from the back or they'll all fall over tonight. Then we'll be ready to go."

Guntzie crawled under the table and worked on the papier-mâché from the back. "There, that ought to do it. How's it look? Wait'll I get out of the way."

"Great. It looks great. When do the judges come?"

Guntzie went to straighten a still life of onions and garlic. "Miss Nichols said they start judging at seven, but even I won't know who won till I see the ribbons after the concert. Are your mother and father coming up with you or do you have to get here early for the Glee Club?"

"I've got to be here by seven. Dad'll come later, but of course Mom has to stay home with the crown prince. Oh, well, so what else is new?"

I turned away quickly and started picking up my books. I was hurt and angry, but suddenly I didn't want to talk about it. Even to Guntzie.

At the door we stopped and looked back. I hugged my books to my chest and shivered inside.

"It is exciting, isn't it?"

"You wait, Dorrie, if you want to know real excitement. Just wait till you have your first one-woman show. That's excitement."

Guntzie and I silently walked home down Madison Avenue. I held her words carefully in my mind as if they might suddenly shatter. I knew Guntzie didn't give out compliments easily. All of a sudden I felt wildly excited. As if . . . really . . . maybe someday—a show of my own.

I punched the elevator button, then ran all the way to the fourth floor. I was in such a good mood I didn't even care that Fredlet had slushed water all over the bathroom and squeezed green toothpaste around the sink. I cleaned up the mess and washed my hair and took a shower. After I was dressed, Mom made me a sandwich and I never once asked her what she had decided about coming to Spring Festival. I didn't want to fight. *Nothing*, absolutely nothing was going to spoil my night. I even had a good feeling about the judges. All at once I was king of the mountain.

Pat called, and she and Ann and I arranged to meet on Ninetieth and Madison and go to school together. By the time we got there, we were caught up in the excitement: makeup, the white choir gowns, the whole bit.

Backstage I could hear the muffled sounds of the audience on the other side of the curtain: chairs scraping, assorted coughs, and the rattle of programs. Mr. Carr, the Glee Club director, signaled to us to take our places. As I climbed to the top row of steps, I held my breath, hoping that the stands were sturdier than they looked. It wasn't the first time I'd wanted to be short and not always in the last row. I took a deep breath and pinched my cheeks as hard as I could.

On the other side of the curtain Miss Hassey began her introduction on the piano. I guess Miss Hassey was everybody's idea of the perpetual accompanist—from the bun on the back of her head to the blue crepe dress with the artificial rose on the bosom. But that night I was so filled with an "all's right with the world" feeling that even old Miss Hassey looked okay to me.

The curtain opened and I could feel the darts of excitement running from girl to girl. The auditorium was small, and as soon as my eyes adjusted to the lights I looked out over the audience. I saw Ann's parents in the very first row, and Miss Nichols next to them nodding encouragement. I saw Guntzie leaning against the wall in the back. Suddenly my voice shook. Right on the aisle, just a few rows back were Mom, Dad, and Fredlet.

I felt myself starting to smile. They had come. All of them. I looked at Fredlet again. He was dressed in his best clothes, his plaid sports coat and a bow tie. His hair was clean and combed. His mouth was shut.

I looked back at Mr. Carr, concentrating on his hands, pronouncing every word distinctly. The program seemed to be flying by, one song after another. Miss Hassey introduced the last group of songs. I breathed deeply, trying to do it quietly so, as Mr. Carr had said, the audience wouldn't feel as though they were being swallowed up by a giant vacuum cleaner. We began "The Battle Hymn of the Republic." The altos sounded strong, the sopranos clear—the way we'd tried to sound in rehearsal and never had.

Suddenly there was a rush of laughter across the room. Mr. Carr snapped his fingers, pinning our attention on himself. I let my eyes sneak out over the audience and my voice froze in my throat. A thousand needles seemed to prickle my body.

Fredlet stood in the aisle, his back to the stage. He swung his arms with majestic clumsiness directing the audience. Occasionally he looked over his shoulder at Mr. Carr, then swung back to copy him. As the song ended and applause filled the room, Fredlet bowed from side to side, then he turned and bowed to us, grinning widely.

I wanted to die—or at least have that shaky platform give way beneath me. I tried to read Mr. Carr's expression, but his face was impassive. "The finale," he whispered. The music started. I moved my lips and I guess sound came out. I don't know, and I don't care. Fredlet walked up and down the aisle waving and nodding.

As the curtain closed on the last curtain call, I sat down on the top step and put my head in my hands. I never planned to move again. Never. Pat came up behind me and said, "Come on. Let's go see who won the art show and get something to eat. I'm sure you won something."

"Oh, you go on. I'll come later. Oh, wasn't he awful? Why did they bring him? I'm humiliated."

"Come on, Dorrie. He wasn't that bad. People enjoy Fredlet. People except you, that is. Come on, I'm hungry."

"You wouldn't enjoy him if he was your brother. I'll bet Mr. Carr's ready to kill me because of the way he ruined the concert."

"He didn't ruin the concert. And Mr. Carr couldn't blame you even if he did, which he didn't anyway. Now come on and just put your head up and let's go. The food will be all gone if we don't hurry."

It was pretty obvious that Pat wasn't going anywhere without me, so I followed her through the auditorium and out into the hall, never taking my eyes off the floor. Miss Nichols stood by the door greeting everyone, and next to her stood Fredlet. Together they formed a grotesque receiving line. His face was red, his bow tie crooked, but he kept bowing and shaking hands.

"A lovely concert, Dorrie. Really lovely," said

Miss Nichols. She smiled and handed me on to Fredlet. "Here's someone waiting for you, I think."

"How do. How do *you* do, Dorrie?" said Fredlet.

"Dorrie, I think your parents are having refreshments and I know they'll be waiting for you. Your brother and I will greet the rest of the guests."

"Yes, Miss Nichols," I muttered, and I could have kissed her right there even though she was the principal. I yanked my hand away from Fredlet and worked my way through the crowd. "Come on," urged Pat. "Let's go see the art prizes first, and then eat. And that's a real sacrifice on my part."

I stopped by the art room. "Pat, wait. Do me a favor, please. Go on to the dining room and tell my parents I have to help Guntzie for a while and I'll come home with her." Pat started to argue but I didn't give her a chance. I turned and started away, calling over my shoulder, "Pat, please, just go."

As I entered the room where the art show was being held, several girls rushed up to me. "Hey, Dorrie, have you seen? Congratulations." I skirted the wall by the ceramics display, hardly daring to look. All around me people kept smiling and nodding like funny mirrors at a carnival. There was the green ceramic cat, and under his front paw was the blue ribbon. One of the seniors came up to me. "Hey, Dorrie, you really cleaned up. First prize in drawing too. That's wild!"

Suddenly I saw Guntzie pushing her way through

the crowd. "Dorrie, congratulations. Miss Nichols said to tell you the judges want to meet you. Let's see if we can work our way back out into the hall."

I followed Guntzie as we snaked our way back across the room. She was little, but her elbows and shoulders seemed sharp and pointed. Guntzie never actually pushed, but a path seemed to open up for her. As we got to the main hall I saw Mom and Dad and Fredlet going down the steps. Guntzie saw them too.

"Look, Dorrie, there goes your family. Did they see your ribbons? Elizabeth—Joe—" she called. Guntzie's voice was lost in the noise of the crowd. "Oh, Dorrie, do you think they saw your prizes?" Someone tapped her on the shoulder and she swung around. I never answered Guntzie's question.

The apartment had that middle-of-the-night feeling even though it was only a little after ten o'clock. "You'd think they'd be waiting up," I thought. "They must have heard about the ribbons." I headed back toward my parents' room. Just as I was about to knock, I pulled back my hand as if it had been scalded. I heard the low rumble of my father's voice. But it was the other sound that made me stop. Never in all the years of my life did I ever remember hearing my mother cry. Until tonight.

I stood in the shadowy hall outside my parents' room. I felt very heavy and somehow tired. In my mind I could see again my mother and father and

Fredlet going down the steps at school—and how I'd never run after them—never taken them in to see my prizes. I listened to my mother cry. Could I have done that? And suddenly I was very frightened to think that possibly something I had done could hurt her that much.

I moved quietly away from the door, not knowing what to do. On the way down the hall I tiptoed into Fredlet's room. I watched him as he lay sleeping on his back, one arm flung over his head, the other bent around his teddy bear. He looked soft and young and easy to hurt. Fredlet slept with his mouth open making adenoid noises. I pulled the cover up over him and looked around the room, not quite ready to leave. I picked up the crumpled sports coat from the floor, hung it on the chair, and went slowly back to my room.

9

Talk about the haves and the have-nots—that May I guess I was the biggest have-not that ever crawled around the face of the earth. True, I had the blue ribbons from the art show, but somehow they didn't seem to mean much anymore. The morning after Spring Festival Mom and Dad had come into my room and said all the right things, and Mom hung the ribbons on the bulletin board in the kitchen right next to Fredlet's scribble-scrabble picture from school. After a few days, the ribbons looked faded and stiff, and I took them down and shoved them in the back of my desk and left them there. The rest of my world felt like the highest block in the stack that Fredlet piled up time after time—swaying and teeter-tottering. And I knew what always happened to Fredlet's blocks. The only question was how long.

Mom and Dad seemed to be having more and more long talks. There were long-distance calls to my grandmother and from aunts and uncles; talk about houses and offices and subletting the apartment. Sometimes I felt as if I were walking on a bunch of rubber bands pulled taut, and any minute one was going to snap. I wanted to know what was going on, but I didn't really want to know. I tried to block it all out. For once I didn't blab to Ann and Pat. I never even said anything to Guntzie, though I knew that she knew from my mother. That was another thing about Guntzie. She left it up to me to say something or not. And I chose not, though I knew I could have if I wanted to, and I guessed I would someday.

Anyway, there I was—the biggest have-not in all of Manhattan—when Pat called about June Week. Mom was out and I was there with Fredlet, and he was on the living-room floor with his fat jumbo crayons and a pad of paper, and I really had to watch him because he wasn't always sure where the paper ended and the walls began—or tables, or lampshades. And why did a kid that big want crayons anyway?

I stretched the phone cord as far down the hall as it would go. "Wait a minute, Pat. I have to get settled again so I can watch Fredlet while we talk. Now tell me again, from the beginning."

"Well," said Pat, "you know Bill—I met him last

summer. We wrote and all, and we went out at Christmas. You know, he's at the Naval Academy. Well, he wrote and invited me down for June Week."

"You're kidding. You never said a word. How come you never said a word?"

"I wanted to make sure my parents would let me go. It took some doing but I talked them into it. Anyway, that's not the point. Bill has a roommate —Jerry—and he had asked a girl from home but she just had her appendix out and now she can't go so he, Jerry, wants Bill to get me to get a friend for him, even though it's awfully late to ask, and that's where you come in. The friend, I mean."

"You're kidding," I screeched. "Me? Really? What's he look like? How old is he? What's his name?"

"His name's Jerry something or other and he's a plebe—a freshman—same as Bill, and I don't know what he looks like but Bill says he's really nice. What do you think? Will your parents let you go?"

I hitched the phone higher on my shoulder. "Oh, gosh, I don't know. You know how they are. I can almost hear them now—'Who is this boy? And who are his parents? What do you mean you want to go to Annapolis? What do you know about him?' Anyway, they've been so queer lately, who knows what they're going to do."

"Well, talk them into it," said Pat. "I could have

my mother call yours. You've just got to go. We'll have the best time."

"I'll ask tonight, but don't let your mother call till I've worked on them awhile."

I helped my mother stack the Rice Krispies in the cupboard and the Ajax under the sink, all the while trying to think of the best way to approach this whole Annapolis thing.

"Hey, Mom, what time will Dad be home?"

"Your father? Your father left for Maryland this morning, Dorrie. He won't be home till Friday night."

"Maryland? Friday night? Nobody ever told me he was going away. What for? I've got to talk to him."

"We did tell you, Dorrie. We talked about it at dinner last night. You must not have been listening."

"Nobody told me. Nobody tells me anything in this house," and the whole time I was saying it I vaguely remembered my father coming into my room the night before while I was involved in a drawing. I sort of remembered the words "and help your mother" and me saying "uh-huh." But right then none of that mattered. "This is Wednesday," I went on, "and Friday's not until—uh—Friday. And I have to talk to him now. What'll I do?"

"Well, I'm here, Dorrie. What do you want to talk to him about anyway?"

I took a deep breath. "Well, there's this boy that

Pat knows—you know, I told you about him—the one she met last summer who goes to the Naval Academy. Well, he has this friend, and he—not the friend, but Bill, Pat's friend, invited her down for June Week—and Jerry—he's Bill's roommate—well, anyway, Jerry's girl had her appendix out and can't go so he—Jerry—needs a date and Pat wants me to go, but I have to know right away so Pat can tell Bill and he can tell Jerry and . . ."

Mom folded the last grocery bag and put it away. "Wait a minute, Dorrie. I can't understand a word you're saying. Start over again—and slower."

"But, Mom, I just did explain it. Okay. Pat. You do know Pat, don't you?"

"All right. Of course I know Pat."

"Well, Pat knows this boy named Bill who goes to the Naval Academy and he invited her down to Annapolis for June Week. Okay?"

"Well, that's nice, I guess," said Mom, dumping ground beef into a bowl.

Fredlet came shuffling into the kitchen holding his catalog by the cover. He flopped down in the middle of the kitchen floor and started flipping pages. "Ma—Ma—look chair." It's almost impossible to have a conversation in our house what with Mom mushing up hamburgers and Fredlet saying, "Chair —Ma—chair" louder and louder.

"That's right, Fred. That's chair," said Mom automatically.

"Mom, you're not listening," I said. "This is important."

"Yes I am, Dorrie. Good Fred—boat. That's right, a boat. You said Pat's going to Annapolis for June Week."

"Ma—Ma. Shoe. See shoe." Fredlet rolled onto his stomach, leaning on his elbows as he turned the pages.

"Oh, for Pete's sake," I exploded. "Why does he keep looking at that stupid catalog. He must have a hundred picture books, and he can't read anyway."

"But he likes the catalog better. He always has," said Mom. "How about setting the table, Dorrie. Since Dad's away we might as well eat early."

"But Mom—about Pat and Bill . . ."

"Bill who?"

"Bill-the-boy-who-asked-Pat-to-June-Week."

"Cookie—cookie," demanded Fredlet, standing on a chair to reach the cupboard.

"No, Fred. No cookie. Get down," said Mom. "All right, Dorrie. What about Pat and Bill?"

"Well, Bill has a friend named Jerry whose date can't go and Bill wants Pat to bring a friend and that's me."

"You mean you want to go to Annapolis for June Week with Pat?" asked my mother like maybe we'd been talking about space exploration on Mars or something.

"Well, yes—go with Pat but really with Bill's

friend Jerry. It's okay, isn't it? I have to call her tonight so she can write Bill and he can tell Jerry and then Jerry's going to write and invite me, okay?"

Then the bomb dropped. "No, it's not one bit okay," said my mother.

"But, Mom, you said it was very nice for Pat to go to June Week."

"Well, maybe it is nice for Pat—but not for you."

Sometimes I absolutely can't believe mothers.

"Well, why not?" I asked.

"Because Pat's not my daughter and you are. I guess that's why."

"But, Mom, Pat's mother thinks it's great. I mean she likes her daughter to do things and have fun."

"Now, Dorrie, you know we like you to do things and have fun too, but you're not quite ready for June Week at the Academy. You're not old enough. Oh, goodness, Fred's asleep on the floor. I hope that doesn't mean he'll be up all night."

"Mo—ther, I'm fifteen years old and I certainly think I'm old enough to do what I want. Everybody else can."

"Dorrie, your father and I've told you a hundred times we don't care about everybody else. They're not our concern. It's only you we have to worry about."

"Well, I don't want to be worried about. I just want to be able to do what everybody else is doing. You don't care about me, anyhow."

"Dorrie, we do care about you. We always have.

And I'm not at all sure that everybody else is doing all these things. There'll be time enough for all this later on."

"Time enough when? I'm tired of hearing how much time I have. Why can't I go now?"

"No, Dorrie. Not this year, and that's final. I don't want to hear any more about it."

"Wake up, Fredlet," I said, giving him a hard poke with my foot. "That's the trouble around here. Nobody wants to hear anything. Will you at least ask Dad when he calls? I mean, he trusts me."

"It's not a matter of trust, Dorrie. I'll mention it to your father, but I'm sure he'll agree with me. Come on, now. Everything's ready. Fred, it's time to eat. Dorrie, will you please get the catsup."

I slammed the catsup down on the table as hard as I dared. "Yeah, it's like a conspiracy around here. And anyway, Annapolis is in Maryland and all of a sudden everybody around here thinks Maryland is so great. And I don't see why Fredlet has to dunk hamburger in his milk. It's disgusting. Anyway, what'll I tell Pat? She promised Bill she'd find a friend for Jerry and she did ask me first."

"Well, she'll just have to ask someone else and that's that. And besides, I'll bet that's the same weekend as your father's law school reunion. I don't much feel like going, but it's been twenty years and he's really counting on it. And with Mrs. Moran laid up we'll need you to stay with Fred." Mom reached over to cut Fredlet's hamburger. I mean, who can't cut a hamburger? "You know, Dorrie, I'm a little concerned about Fred lately. He doesn't seem to have much pep. Maybe I'll have Dr. Weinberg take a look at him."

There she went again—my mother, I mean—not wanting to go to the reunion, but worrying about Fred. If I ever get married, and if I ever have kids, which I sort of doubt, I'm never going to stop wanting to go places—all different—and seeing everything.

"Dorrie," my mother said, breaking into my thoughts, "why don't you call Pat now so she'll have time to get someone else."

That did it. I mean, it was bad enough not to be able to go to June Week and to have to call Pat and tell her—but then to have to stay with Fredlet besides. I banged my fork down and slammed away from the table. As I ran down the hall I could hear Fredlet starting to yell, "Poor Dorrie—all gone. Poor Cat. Hamburger—more."

For the next two days my eyes felt like burning coals. I cried a lot. And then to have to call Pat, who was actually pretty nice about it, but, of course, I knew what she was thinking—even though I told her all about my father's reunion and how I had to take care of Fredlet or otherwise I'd be sure to go. And, of course, I knew then she'd asked Ann and she was going (even though her mother was really strict), and if I hadn't liked them so much I would have hated them.

When I let myself into the apartment Friday afternoon after school, well, actually after after-school-at-Schrafft's, I heard my father's voice coming from the kitchen. His voice sounded lighter and more the way it used to than it had in a long time. I heard my mother laugh. I knew that was a bad sign. I leaned my head on the woodwork in the hall, wondering if I could get to my room without Mom or Dad knowing I was home. Words spun around me. "You know the old Bennett house." "Our luck that it's on the market." "A wonderful garden." "A swing for Fred."

I had made it halfway to my room when my mother called. "Dorrie, is that you? Come in the kitchen, Dad's back early."

"Come on," called my father. "I have some exciting news."

10

My mother was on the floor. She had dumped two shoe boxes of snapshots on the linoleum and was rummaging through them. Getting the snapshots out of the shoe boxes and into an album was something my mother was always going to do, or I was going to do for her. We never did.

Anyway, there was Mom on her hands and knees with her glasses pushed up on the top of her head—and the way she was going at those pictures was really weird. She looked like a little kid. And there was my father bending over her, saying, "Try that pile over there. They have to be here. I remember those pictures." And Mom said, "I had a new yellow dress for that party, remember? I took it on our honeymoon."

I sat down at the kitchen table and felt like I was made of lead all the way through. Suddenly I felt a hundred and ten years old and as if I was the Earth

Mother or something. Or at least the mother of my mother and father, and that maybe I should say, "Put your toys away right now and go and wash your hands." Instead I asked, "What are you looking for?"

They both looked up surprised, and I thought I could probably have made it to my room after all. "Oh, hi," said Mom. "Remember those pictures taken years ago when the Bennetts gave the party for your father and me before we were married? I'm sure you've seen them."

"Look, here they are," said Dad, and his voice sounded like he'd found the prize in the box of Cracker Jacks. "You can see the porch in this one. And here's the backyard. The trellis is gone now, but it's pretty much the same."

Mom was up from the floor and looking over his shoulder. "Oh, it is a nice house. Look, come here. You remember Mrs. Bennett's house. You've been there with Grandma, I'm sure. That's your father's news."

"Yeah, I remember," I said out of my leaden mouth on my leaden face. Dad looked at me funny. "But that's the house. *Our* house, or it almost is. Mrs. Bennett has stayed there ever since her husband died, but now she's going to Richmond and will take an apartment near her daughter and son-in-law. And she's so glad we're buying the house."

"I practically grew up in that house," my mother went on. "Ellen Bennett was my best friend for years and years. She was our maid of honor—that's what the party was all about. Dorrie, you haven't said a word. Here, look at these pictures—just pretend the people aren't in them. Look, see that window, that was Ellen's room and it will be great for you. You go down two steps to get to the room and there's a den connected to it. I always loved that room, and you will too." I hadn't heard my mother talk that much in ages. She just kept going. "And look at that corner; that would be a great room for Fred. And the yard will be so good for him. How about a swing? And I'll have a garden."

"I'm not much of a gardener," said Dad, "but I hope I can keep Mrs. Bennett's roses going. Well, Dorrie, what do you think?"

"I'm not going." First I said it just blah—just said it, and my mother and father were all set to keep talking—gardens—swings—yards. As if I could care.

"I'm *not going ever*. I'm not and you can't make me. I don't care what you do. . . ." I started out of the kitchen.

"Dorrie." My father's voice was like a shot. "Sit down."

I sat down.

"Ma—Ma. Come Ma." Fredlet called in a sleepy voice.

"Oh dear, Fred fell asleep after school. I'd better see what he wants." Mom dropped the pictures on the table and hurried out of the room. Her knuckles hit the door as she went out and that sound echoed through the room. It was a dull and heavy sound.

I looked at the picture of the house and hated it. I tried to fit myself in somewhere, but it didn't work. That house wasn't me. I belonged here—where I was—in New York. I could almost taste the wonderful things I was going to do. The one-woman show I was going to have one day, living in my own studio, seeing my own paintings in the Museum of Modern Art—maybe even the Guggenheim. Things that had nothing to do with Mrs. Bennett's roses or Fredlet's swing. "But, Dad, I—I'm . . ."

"Dorrie, keep quiet and listen. I think it's all very well to get everyone's opinion in a family, everyone who's able to have an opinion, that is." And I knew he was thinking of Fredlet, and his shoulders sagged. Dad went on, "And I think it's important to talk things out, and God knows we've talked; and to weigh all sides, and I think you'll have to admit we've done that. But there comes a time when a decision has to be made—and that decision has been made. For the overall good of this family we're moving to Tunbridge. And that's final. Decision made."

"Overall good, my foot," I screamed. "For Fredlet's good," and I started out of the kitchen.

"Sit down. For once you're not going to run out of the room. You're going to sit and listen." Dad walked across the kitchen and looked down the areaway. "Yes, for Fred's good, but Fred's good affects your mother's good, and mine, and even yours whether you know it or not."

"It doesn't. Not in any way. Fredlet's Fredlet and I'm me and—"

"And he's your brother"—my father's voice was hard and flat—"and he's mentally retarded and there's nothing on God's earth you can do to change that. And it's not the worst thing in the world. Not by a long shot."

"Dad, how can you say—"

"Look around you. You want to be an artist. An artist has to see, see it all. Sure we have a problem, most people do. And right now our best way of handling this problem is to get Fred, and all of us, out of the city. If it's at all possible, your mother and I will try to work something out for you."

I felt hard as nails. I didn't care. Nothing my father said even touched me. I scooped the pictures up and put them back into the boxes and buried the ones of the Bennett house underneath. I didn't want to see them again. Ever. Icing my voice with sarcasm, I said, "May I have your permission to leave now? I mean, if it's for the overall good of the family I have work to do in Guntzie's studio. If it would suit the honorable family."

My father never turned from the window. "Go on. Go on and go." His voice sounded old and empty. I knew I'd done that and I didn't care. I went anyway.

Looking back to that day in Guntzie's studio is like looking at an Impressionist painting, maybe a Monet. There is little that's clear-cut—mostly dabs, hazes. Well, an impression, I guess.

I'm sure Guntzie got an earful. All the "it's not fair," "what are they trying to do," "I won't," "they can't make me."

Somewhere in the middle I remember her calling home and telling my mother I'd be back after supper. And I guess I remember supper. I'm not sure. I remember scrubbing the linoleum, and cleaning crocks, and throwing away empty paint tubes. As I said before, Guntzie is a great believer in working out hostilities.

After we ate, Guntzie handed me a dishrag and pointed to the sink.

"You wash and I'll dry."

I ran the water full force. "Okay. I'm sorry. I guess I was pretty awful."

Guntzie shrugged and picked up the dish towel. "You're right. But maybe now that you're calmer we can make some sense out of this."

"You mean out of me." I tried to smile.

"Okay, out of you. But you could have been me, years ago. Nobody ever wanted to come to New York as much as I did."

"But you made it. You're here. You have everything."

Guntzie put the dishes in the cupboard over the sink. "Yes, I have 'everything,' as you put it. When

I was young and back in the mountains there wasn't anything I wanted more than to come to New York and study. To live. And I did. Much against my family's wishes. I came. And once I was here it was awfully easy not to go back. More and more I didn't go—I didn't need them."

I wrung out the rag and hung it over the faucet. Guntzie took another cup of coffee and we sat down at the table. I never remembered hearing Guntzie really talk about herself before.

"Did they get used to the idea—of your being in New York, I mean?"

"Not really. But it wasn't New York. My sister moved to California and that was all right. But she kept in touch. I was so determined to be independent I guess you could say I shut myself off. It doesn't have to be that way. I know that now."

"But if something's important to you—and it is important to me to stay in New York and not go to Maryland . . ."

"I know it's important, and I hope something works out for you. But it's the art that's important. You've got to believe that. Art in New York or Maryland or East Podunk. But don't pull away too much—from your family—even from Fredlet."

Guntzie lit another cigarette and folded a paper napkin in triangles over and over. The veins stood out on the back of her hands. "I'm lecturing you and I don't mean to."

"Do you still see them? Your family, I mean?" I felt funny asking about people I'd never even known existed.

"My parents are dead," said Guntzie. She got up quickly and took the dulcimer off the wall. Sitting down, she laid it across her lap and started to pluck the strings—both hands moving quickly at first, then slower until she was almost coaxing the melody out. To me the dulcimer sounded like a little bit of banjo and bagpipe, with some zither thrown in. It was a faraway mountain sound. And Guntzie's eyes had a distant look. Her fingers pulled at the notes.

"I see my sister sometimes," she went on. "If I'm in California I drop in and do the aunt bit for a while. But it's not really good. It never works. It's been too long."

The music ran over me like water. Guntzie went from "Frankie and Johnny" to "The Ash Grove" and then to exercises. Even the exercises were haunting. Something deep inside of me ached.

"Maybe that's why I like you Shafers so much. You give me a lot."

"Who? Us? What could we give to anybody? What with Fredlet the way he is, and me always mad, and Mom and Dad so sort of—we're hardly what you'd call perfect."

Guntzie laughed. "No, not perfect, but okay. Would you want them to be perfect?" She got up and put the dulcimer aside, then poured some more coffee. "Remember last year when we went to that superrealism show? Remember what you thought of it?"

"Yes—I didn't like it. It was too—I don't know. Too—exact, maybe."

"Right. Maybe things really look like that—but they're not. And we know that. Take your family, for instance. In superrealism, almost a photograph—they're not really real—but flat. Now pretend you're doing an abstract of them."

I closed my eyes instinctively, trying to see my family in abstract.

"Take something away. Abstract something. Maybe you'd say it was distorted a little, but isn't it more real?"

I nodded my head slowly.

"Take away the greeting-card mother and father —the too perfect brother and sister."

I opened my eyes. Guntzie was using her hands again—blocking out my "family" in the air. She went on, "Distort the relationship a little. You're not weakening it—you're strengthening it. Just because your 'family' doesn't look like something out of Fredlet's Sears catalog doesn't mean it isn't valid. And you're part of the picture, Dorrie. Don't be too independent. We all need someone sometime. A way of reaching out. Maybe that's what the Shafers are to me—and the kids at Miss Benson's." Guntzie stood up. "And that's the end of the sermonizing for the night. Philosophy by Guntz. Now go home."

And oddly enough I felt better. Guntzie hadn't said half the things I'd wanted her to say. There hadn't been buckets of sympathy, but she had let me scream and holler for a while. I think it was the first time I realized that it was possible to be absolutely one hundred percent miserable and not have someone wipe it away with a Kleenex. And she had listened, and listening counts for a lot.

As I waited for the elevator I heard my father coming down the stairs. I punched the elevator button again and hurried in as soon as the door slid open. I wasn't quite ready to see Dad yet.

Up in the apartment I went to look for my mother. I heard the shower running in her bathroom and headed for the living room.

"Poor Cat. Poor Cat. Cat up. Cat down." I heard Fredlet's voice and the squeak of the footstool being pulled across the floor. "Poor Cat up."

"Fredlet," I cried from the doorway, "put that down." He swung around on the footstool, and stood swaying in red pajamas, arms outstretched with the green cat almost to the top shelf of the bookcase.

"Fredlet, put it down right now."

Fredlet lurched and grabbed hold of the shelf. The cat hit the floor and shattered.

"You idiot," I shrieked. "You Idiot. Idiot. Idiot. Idiot."

I could hear the word. I could hear my voice. The word bounced around the room—idiot—idiot—

idiot—like some crazy nightmare. I saw my father and Guntzie standing at one door looking at me. I saw my mother wrapped in a yellow robe at the other door with tears running down her face. I saw Fredlet. He had climbed down and was squatting on the floor pushing bits of broken pottery together with his hands. "Poor Cat all gone. Idiot. Fredlet idiot—idiot—idiot," he sang.

I pushed past my father and ran out of the apartment and down the steps and out into the street.

11

All the nighttime demons of New York wouldn't have dared bother me that night. I'm not sure how many times I went around the block, or how many blocks I went around. Somewhere jiggling in the back of my mind I heard years of "stay off the streets at night," "you can't be too careful."

I didn't care what happened to me. What difference would it make? Nothing I did was important—being elected class president or winning the ribbons at the art show. And now the cat was gone—smashed.

I knew I was crying. I could feel the tears on my face. Great silent tears. My jaws ached from clenching them, and my chest felt as if it would burst from unscreamed screams.

Great tearing anger beat inside of me. Anger at Fredlet, and at my mother for loving him so much, and at myself for not loving him enough. And at that stupid cat, which was more valuable to me than a Ming vase. I was mad.

And I was scared.

I could still see my father's face, and I wasn't quite sure I wanted to see it again for a while—maybe ever. Dad didn't get mad often. That's what made it harder. Sort of the *x* in the algebra problem.

I walked. Somewhere in the background there was traffic, and doormen. Once I even walked into a fireplug—and cursed the bruises on my shins. I think I cried some more.

I don't know if I was really going anywhere, but I ended up at Pat's and that worked out pretty well because Ann was there too. Actually they were planning their trip to Annapolis but were nice enough not to say so.

I was shaking by the time I got inside even though the night was warm, and Pat made hot chocolate and we sat around the kitchen table and I told them everything—about moving and not being there next year, about the fight with my parents, and a little bit about yelling at Fredlet because he broke my cat. But I couldn't bring myself to tell them what I'd called him.

They gave me all the sympathy that Guntzie hadn't. They understood. They knew I was right and they told me so.

"Oh, Dorrie, that's the worst thing I've ever heard."

"You ought to count as much as Fredlet."

"You'd think they could wait two more years."

"I can't see you in a small town. It's not you."

"Your father always seems so calm. Now, if it were mine . . ."

And pretty soon I was crying, and so was Ann. And Pat said, "Hey, cut that out, you two. We can't figure anything out that way."

"Figure what out?" I asked.

"About next year, of course. You just can't go. Hey, you could live here. My mother wouldn't mind." And as much as I didn't care whether my mother cared or not I could just hear her saying, "It's a shame about Pat's mother. She has a drinking problem, you know." And right away I knew that wouldn't work.

Then Ann said, "Oh, Dorrie, you could stay at our place. It'd be fun." But somehow I didn't think anything much was fun at Ann's. I mean, her father wasn't too well, and Ann's mother seemed to have enough trouble with Ann and her brother, not to mention the old grandmother.

And for some reason all that made me cry harder, but I couldn't say why, so I muttered something about being afraid to go home, and after a while I really began believing it. Then I thought how my parents must be really worried by then and how that served them right.

"Your father wouldn't beat you, would he?" asked Ann.

"He—he might," I choked, and suddenly I had an awful daytime nightmare of a man with a big leather strap, but he wasn't my father—but he was—or might have been. Then I felt worse. I knew as well as I knew my name that my father would never touch me. But I'd said he might beat me, and I couldn't unsay it—I wouldn't.

"You're not going home tonight, and that's that," said Pat. "You're going to spend the night here. I guess you'd better call your mother and tell her, but I'm not sure why."

Pat reached for a stack of graham crackers. She always thought better while eating.

"I can't call. I just can't. What am I going to say?"

"Well, we'll call, then. You want to do it, Ann? Go ahead, just tell whoever answers that Dorrie's upset and has gone to bed."

Ann looked not quite sure. "Okay, I guess. What'll I do if they want to talk to Dorrie, though?"

"I told you," said Pat, "she's asleep. That's easy. Now go on, here, I'll dial for you."

I held my breath until I heard my father answer the phone. He sounded loud and firm and not at all worried. Ann began to stutter. "Un—uh—Mr. Shafer—this is Ann Hernandez—uh, you know—Dorrie's friend. Well, I'm calling to tell you that Dorrie's at Pat's and she's upset and now she's asleep, so she'll be home tomorrow."

"Put Dorrie on the phone."

"But—but, Mr. Shafer, she's . . ."

"Ann, please put Dorrie on the phone."

Ann handed me the phone. "H-hello," and I was furious with the way my voice came out all scared and little.

"Dorrie, I will expect you in this apartment in ten minutes. Since your friends seem so understanding I suggest you ask them to walk you home. Good-bye."

And there I was holding a silent telephone.

"Oh, you poor thing. What are you going to do?"

"I have to go," I said, pushing away from the table, and suddenly I wanted to shake off their sympathy the way a dog shakes off his coat. I was very, very tired.

My father opened the apartment door as soon as the elevator stopped. He followed me to my room. "Get to bed, Dorrie. You look all in. Too much sympathy never agrees with anyone, but just for the record you're grounded through next weekend."

As soon as he left I ran to the bathroom and threw up. Then I fell into bed and slept better than I had in weeks.

The whole next week felt almost like summer, and I had a lot of time to enjoy it—from my window. And a lot of time to study for exams. Being grounded had certain advantages, like giving me an excuse to avoid my two best friends when they wanted to know how my monster parents were, long past the time when I'd figured out that Mom and Dad weren't the monsters, and that maybe, just maybe, I was.

Being grounded gave me more time in the studio. Guntzie never mentioned Friday night, but when I started work on another cat and said, "This one's for Fredlet," she looked at me like maybe there was hope. For me, I mean.

One day, in the middle of the week, Mom and I took Fredlet to the park. We started around the reservoir with Fredlet dragging a stick along the metal fence and the stick going clink—clink—clink. We could always only go a little way around and then had to turn back because Fredlet got tired. I don't think I ever did get all the way around that reservoir. And lately it seemed we had to sit down and rest—longer and longer.

"Dorrie," Mom said, "we have news for you. Dad and Guntzie and I."

"What? What kind of news?"

"We know, all of us, how much it means for you to be with your class, and stay in New York, so Guntzie's offered to let you stay with her for the next two school years and finish up at Miss Benson's."

I felt like a goldfish. I just stood there opening and closing my mouth. Finally I found my voice.

"Do you mean it?" I screeched. "Really? You're not kidding? Did Guntzie really say I could? And it's all right with you and Dad?"

I couldn't stand still. I grabbed Fredlet's hand and tried to pull him along the cinder path.

"Come on, Fredlet. Let's run. Let's dance. Let's do something. I'm so happy I could scream."

"Oh, Dorrie," laughed my mother, "slow down, you'll hurt him."

"But I'm so happy." I wanted to shout.

"I'm glad. We all are. You'll go down with us in a couple of weeks and you can come up by train in September."

I could hardly stand still long enough to listen to my mother.

"Okay. Sure. Whatever you say. Now can I go back? I want to see Guntzie. You're sure? She really did say I could stay?"

"I'm positive. Run along now. We'll see you at home."

And I did run—out of the park, down Fifth Avenue to Ninetieth, then over to Madison. It was a good kind of running—like being five years old and at a picnic.

Guntzie was mixing paint when I got there.

"Is it true?" I asked. "Did you really say I could stay here? Do you mean it?" I finally had to stop and catch my breath.

"I don't say things I don't mean," said Guntzie, taking the palette to the window to check the blue she had mixed.

"But that's so great. I mean—I mean—well—thank you I guess is what I mean."

"You may not think it's so great next year," she said, adding more yellow to the daub of paint. "Living with me won't be easy, at best. I'm a real ogre at times, and you must promise me one thing."

"Anything," I said.

"Never, never, never speak to me early in the morning or when I'm working. And you know what that extra room of mine looks like—not much bigger than a broom closet. I don't know where you'll put your stuff. And another thing—I'll make you work. You know that, don't you? And when you have dates I'll give them all the third degree. You may be sorry you ever stayed."

"Okay to everything. And I'll even promise not to play my records too loud."

"Oh, good grief. I forgot about the records. Maybe I'll be the one wishing you'd gone to Maryland," she said, laughing. "Now go home and let me work."

That night I glazed Fredlet's cat. This time I pushed the green aside and chose yellow. There's something about yellow. I mean, it's so alive and full of hope.

12

From the living-room window I looked down Madison Avenue as far as I could see and suddenly felt as though I was living one of those strange books where only a few people are left in the world and I was one of them, but hadn't found the others yet. I've never been really sure where all New Yorkers go on summer weekends. They can't all go to Connecticut or Long Island.

Well, Ann and Pat were at the Naval Academy, and Mom and Dad were at the Waldorf hotel for Dad's law school reunion, and Fredlet had gone to bed early, and I guess Guntzie was downstairs. And I felt bored and empty and didn't know what to get into. TV was all reruns, and I couldn't sit still long enough to read, and I wasn't in the mood to draw, and I was out of clay. The yellow cat had been fired and the kiln in Guntzie's apartment had been cooling since the night before and would be ready to unload, but I didn't dare leave Fredlet long enough to run get it.

Mom had put boxes in my room, and I wandered in to start packing them. I began sorting through the stuff on my bureau but somehow couldn't get anything into the boxes. I fingered the half-empty cologne bottles, the plastic champagne glass, the paper flowers. I bent the earring tree back into shape and hung all the earrings through the little holes, then rearranged my jewelry box. Going through the ceramic mug, I picked at little cakes of motel soap, stray beads, and a half-used tube of Clearasil. Then I blew the dust off the top of the chest and went on to the bookcase.

It ought to be easy to pack books, I thought, sitting down on the floor. I yanked a handful of books off the top shelf and found my old diaries and autograph books from grade school behind them. I started reading out loud, but the stuff was so queer, and there wasn't anybody to read it to, or laugh with, so I threw the books in the box and went to get a Coke.

"If only I could get the cat," I thought. I knew I could do it in five minutes. I looked at my watch. Fredlet had been asleep for over an hour and he hardly ever woke up at night. Taking the apartment key off the hook, I started for the door, but stopped at Fredlet's room just to make sure he was asleep so I wouldn't have to rush.

Something was wrong with Fredlet.

As soon as I pushed open the door I could hear him, and in the light from the hall I could see that his eyes were wide open, and scared, and they never left my face. His arms flopped back and forth at his side, reaching for air. I switched on the light and knelt beside him. His face was shiny with sweat and his lips were blue.

"Fredlet, Fredlet, what's the matter? Tell Dorrie." I tried to catch one of his restless hands. I tried to stop the shaking inside me. Fredlet's eyes got wider and wider.

I held his head between my hands and spoke to him. "Look, Fredlet, it's Dorrie. You'll be all right. Dorrie's going to call Dr. Weinberg and I'll be right back. Fredlet, don't be scared, everything's going to be all right." I pushed myself away from the bed and tried not to run till I got out in the hall, praying all the way that Dr. Weinberg hadn't gone to Connecticut or Long Island.

Grabbing the address book off the kitchen shelf, I dialed Dr. Weinberg's number. His voice when he answered was warm and strong.

"Dr. Weinberg, this is Dorrie Shafer. I'm here with Fredlet and he's really sick. He's gasping and all sweaty and his lips are bluer than I've ever seen them, and—and he's scared. He's so very scared."

"All right, Dorrie. Listen carefully. I take it you're alone with Fred?"

"Yes—yes."

"Go back and stay with him, keep talking to him,

and I'll send an ambulance and meet you at the hospital."

I held on to Fredlet's hands and I talked. I told him all about the new yellow cat and how it was for him, and I talked about the new house, and the swing, and how we were going to ride the train to Maryland, and how the train wheels said, "Got your trunk—got your trunk," and a lot of other stuff.

The ambulance men were quick and kind, but still Fredlet's eyes got bigger. They lifted him onto the stretcher and let me stay beside him and hold his hand as they pushed him onto the elevator. Until a door at the end of the hall opened I felt I really was in a deserted world. Mrs. Duncan looked out. "Dorrie, what's wrong? Can I help?"

"My parents—they're at the Waldorf at a law school reunion. Would you go down and ask Miss Guntz to call them, please."

Outside, the ambulance was parked at the curb, the back open, the light blinking. The men slid the stretcher in and I climbed in front. Catching the driver by the sleeve, I said, "Uh, I don't know if you can, but the siren—it really hurts his ears and it scares him."

"Okay, I'll do what I can. The city's quiet tonight, maybe we won't need it." As the ambulance pulled away I saw Guntzie running toward us with Mrs. Duncan behind her.

From then on it was like some hideous kind of discothèque. Strobe lights blinking. Glaring white lights of the emergency room. Cold green walls. Stainless steel. Doors popping open as the stretcher was wheeled across the mat. The strange twistings of doctors and nurses. Dr. Weinberg waiting at the desk, taking charge.

The woman at the desk had a wart on her chin and asked funny questions and my mind went blank. Fredlet was sick and she wanted to know where my mother was born. I couldn't think. The intercom kept up a steady wail. I closed my eyes and leaned on the desk and the same awful scenes flashed before me.

A nurse tapped me on the arm. "Are you all right?" Then she spoke to the woman of the funny questions and the warty chin. "Dr. Weinberg wants Miss Shafer back with her brother. He says the parents are on their way and you can get the rest of the information from them."

The nurse led me through the crowd in the emergency room, through people with staring eyes and hurt bodies I tried not to see but will never forget.

Fredlet was in a little room where the oxygen made a hissing sound and Dr. Weinberg stood next to the stretcher adjusting the mask on Fredlet's face. Fredlet's hands were quiet and his eyes half-closed. I stood there for a few minutes with my hand on his, then Dr. Weinberg motioned me outside.

"He's doing better, Dorrie. In a little while we'll get him up to intensive care. Can you call and see if anyone got in touch with your parents?"

"Yes, I'll call Guntzie, our neighbor. He'll be all right, you think?" Dr. Weinberg patted me on the shoulder and pointed me toward the pay phone across the hall. As an afterthought he reached into his pocket and handed me a dime.

I dropped the dime and had to crawl under the seat among cigarette butts to find it. I had to think hard to remember Guntzie's number.

Closed in the phone booth, away from sound, I could tell something had happened. It was all in pantomime. People running into Fredlet's room. Dr. Weinberg coming around the corner. I dropped the phone and opened the door.

"Dr. Blue—Dr. Blue—come to emergency."

"Dr. Blue."

A nurse with a machine of some kind disappeared into Fredlet's room. I tried to follow her. The room seemed crowded with some kind of ritual dance. I couldn't see my brother.

Another nurse blocked the door, pushing me back. "Not right now. He's having a little trouble breathing and we're trying to help him. There isn't room now. Please wait outside."

I leaned against the wall opposite Fredlet's room. I leaned on that wall as if my very life depended on it. Someone offered me a chair, someone else suggested the waiting room, a glass of water. I wouldn't move.

A man with a bloody foot stood at the door of the next cubicle; stood with his wife and watched me watch Fredlet's door. I wanted to bloody his other foot and scream, "Get back inside and leave me alone. Let me watch for Fredlet alone, you nosy old fool."

The door opened and the nurse with the machine came out and headed down the hall. Other nurses and doctors came out and melted away. No one looked at me except Mr. and Mrs. Bloody Foot.

Dr. Weinberg came out and closed the door. He looked across the hall and shook his head and put out his hands to me. "We did our best, Dorrie, the whole team. We couldn't save him. He isn't scared anymore."

Dr. Weinberg put his arm around my shoulder and we turned and walked down the hall. I saw my mother and father running toward us.

13

Gradually the names and faces began to stick together—kind of mix and match.

In my head were Aunts Sudie, Julia, Ellen; Uncles Stanley, Thomas, and Truitt; Great-Aunts Grace and Aggie. Andy and Joseph, who were cousins, I thought, the same as Maggie, Ruth, and Geraldine. From somewhere came the names Mrs. Wilkins, and Mrs. Bennett, and the Waddells.

I stood on the hard, dry ground of the cemetery, already scorched and it was only June, and tried to tack the names onto the faces clumped around. More and more cars lined the road and people came across to that awful empty hole, that mound of dirt draped in fake grass, the coffin that was Fredlet—suspended there—the way we were all suspended, and had been for the last few days—and maybe always would be. I wasn't sure.

There was a lot to remember. A jumble. Maybe I'll never sort it out. I guess what I'll remember most about my mother and father was that they kept worrying about me. Me—Dorrie. I mean, there they were, coming down that hall in the hospital, and they had to know their son was dead, and they worried about me.

"Is she all right, Doctor? Dorrie, we're sorry you were here alone." And they put their arms around me and took me home.

There were phone calls that went on into the night, and train schedules, and talks with the New York funeral directors who talked to the Maryland funeral director because of course Fredlet had to go back to Maryland because of the grandmother and the aunts and the great-aunts and the uncles whose names I couldn't match with their faces.

And the trip on the train. The wheels did say, "Got your trunk—got your trunk—got your trunk," and I tried not to listen, but I had to. Then I tried to get them to say something else, but they said, "Got your trunk—got your trunk" all the way through that long, flat trip. And I remembered telling Fredlet about the wheels—and how when I was seven Grandma had told me the wheels say, "Got your trunk."

There was Grandma on the platform, with Aunts Nellie and Ann (I knew those faces). And we kissed and said hello and tried not to see the hearse pulled up next to the brown-box station, and tried not to see what was being taken out of the freight car up front. Till my mother turned and walked toward the men working, and we followed her because it was easier than watching—and she put her hand on the top of the coffin for just a minute. And then we went home, to my grandmother's. And that's all there was.

That's all there was as far as funeral, I mean, until what we were all waiting for there in the cemetery. Mom and Dad had said right away there was to be no wake, no awful staring at Fredlet who wasn't Fredlet anymore, no coming into church, no flowers in the shape of anything.

"God will understand," my mother had said, as if to explain it to Grandma and the aunts. "We want it simple. We want it outside."

Last night the people had come, some with cakes and salads. And there was a ham, and country butter. And that's when I first tried to match names and faces.

"Dorrie, come meet your cousin Gerry."

"Do you remember me, Dorrie? I've known you since you were this big."

"Looks like her grandfather, I think."

"Favors Joe's side."

"She has her mother's eyes."

"Speak loudly to Great-Aunt Aggie. She's deaf, you know."

"Your grandmother says you draw well, Dorrie. I still have a painting your mother did for me. In my parlor all these years."

"I don't guess you have any of your work with you? No, of course you wouldn't."

And all of a sudden I remembered the brown wrapped package that Guntzie had brought up to me as we were leaving our apartment for the train. "Here, Dorrie, it came out really well. You'll be pleased. I thought you might want to take it with you, but I'm not sure why."

And all the way down in the train I held the lumpy package that was Fredlet's yellow cat and never opened it and listened to the wheels say, "Got your trunk—got your trunk."

The minister made his way across the graveyard. My grandmother brought him up to my mother and father. He was young and newly arrived from North Carolina and wouldn't know who favored whom.

He stood at the foot of that awful hole and I can't remember what he said but I remember that I liked it; that it made me think of Fredlet, and that the hole didn't seem as deep anymore, or as dark.

Then he said, "Weep but a little for the dead for he is at rest," and he looked at my mother and father and said, "Fred is at rest."

After that I never thought of Fredlet as Fredlet again, but only as Fred—the way Mom and Dad had always known he was.

14

M̲y mother broke like the weather.

I guess I should have known it would happen. You can't just keep on holding things together forever, like Alice at a perpetual Mad Hatter's tea party. After the funeral there were more relatives, and chicken salad on finger rolls and cucumber sandwiches—and my mother going from group to group smiling and making people feel that that was exactly where they should be, and wasn't everything fine. After they left she put on cotton slacks and an old shirt and went out and pruned the roses. Just like any Monday.

By dinner time the sky was dark, with barely held-up clouds. The Tiffany lamp over the dining-room table spread gold light across the shadows. My grandmother's Tiffany lamp went all the way back to when Tiffany lamps were in, and then out, and now back again and in just about half the restaurants I'd seen. But in my grandmother's house it really belonged.

Anyway, we were pulling up to the table—my grandmother and mother and father, Aunt Nellie and Uncle Truitt, and cousin Geraldine—and my mother said, "Move down, everyone, make room for Fred."

And all of a sudden everyone stopped scraping chairs and talking, and a silence crowded the room until my grandmother sat down at the head of the table and said, "Come on, everyone. My goodness, the hot things will get cold and the cold things hot. Sit down, sit down." But still my mother stood behind her chair and said, "But, Fred, where's my Fred?"

Outside, the lightning streaked across the sky and the rain pounded down. My mother screamed and then started to cry. She huddled against the wall looking little and hurt. Dad led her out of the room and we could hear her sobs all the way up the stairs. And my father's voice, quiet and reasoning.

Grandma smiled brightly and said, "Elizabeth will be fine, just fine. It was bound to happen. She's been a rock." But I noticed she picked at her chicken just like the rest of us.

"You all go on to the dessert without me," said Grandma. "I'll just slip upstairs and see what I can do." The storm howled, and I felt as though the very house shook beneath me.

My grandmother was little and birdlike and she

always wore high heels. Pretty soon I heard her click down the front stairs and use the telephone in the hall. Coming into the dining room, she said, "I just spoke to Thomas and he's coming over to see Elizabeth. He'll give her something to quiet her. What she needs now is rest."

"Thomas? Who's that?" I asked.

"Oh, Dorrie, I keep forgetting it will take time for you to get the family straight. Uncle Thomas is Sudie's husband, and one of the two doctors in town. He just lives in the next block. Believe it or not, down here doctors still do make house calls. Especially for family."

Uncle Thomas came in the rain, carrying an enormous umbrella and wearing a yellow slicker. There was much going up and down the stairs—quiet voices behind closed doors. While Nellie, Geraldine, and I cleaned up the kitchen, Grandma came down for tea and toast, but she hurried back upstairs before we had a chance to ask her anything. After the dishes were done I went into the room my grandfather had always used as an office. The room was almost round, with windows on all sides except where the room hooked onto the house. I sat down in the old Morris chair and watched the rain.

I felt frightened and deserted.

And angry.

I felt like a child—angry because my mother seemed to have abandoned me. I missed Fred, and suddenly I wanted to sit down next to him and look at his Sears, Roebuck catalog with him, even though it was vintage 1964. For a minute I almost thought I could do it. Then I remembered. Then I was mad because he'd gone away and seemed to have taken my mother with him—the way he always had before. But deep down I knew that wasn't true either.

I wandered around the little office. My grandfather's yellow rolltop desk was still against the wall. On top of the glass-fronted bookcase stood a stuffed squirrel and a stuffed pheasant. I remembered as a little girl how I'd like to sit on Grandpa's lap and pat the animals, and talk to them. But now they revolted me. They were no longer playthings. They were dead, and dead things reminded me of Fred. And all of a sudden, in a great flash of lightning, I thought I saw Fred on top of the bookcase—with the squirrel and the pheasant. I ran out of the room.

The next few days were muffled in whispers and tiptoes. Uncle Thomas stopped in every day. There were trays taken to the second floor, and cakes and cookies brought to the door. Every time I looked into my mother's room she seemed to be asleep, with her head turned toward the wall. After a few days, my father had to go back to New York to wind things up at the office. And then I felt even more alone. I think way in the back of my mind I had thought that now that Fred was dead maybe Mom and Dad would decide to stay in New York. But when Dad talked about his new office with Uncle Stanley, and Grandma took me over to see the empty Bennett house, I knew that nothing had changed. No miracle was going to make life the way it used to be.

The days seemed hot and endless. There was nowhere to go. The aunts and cousins asked me to lunches, but on either side of the meal stretched long, boring hours. I prowled Grandma's attic, or garret, as she called it, leafing through scrapbooks and old trunks. I went down to Memorial Library and couldn't believe it was only open three days a week. The library was in an old church with yellow-brown floors and stained-glass windows, and two steps up to the fiction section where the altar used to be. I missed the New York Public Library with the great stone lions out front.

I picked out tunes with one finger on Grandma's piano, and tried to draw but couldn't.

One morning, after breakfast, I went to get my mother's tray and she was propped up on pillows with her eyes open.

"Dorrie, come in. I have deserted you, haven't I? I was so tired. So tired."

"Hi, Mom, can I get you some more coffee?"

For some reason I felt embarrassed seeing my mother. I didn't know what to say.

"Oh, Dorrie, I'd love another cup. Why don't you get yourself a Coke and come up and sit with me."

I gave Mom her coffee and went to sit in a rocker by the window.

"Uh, are you feeling better? I mean, are you rested?"

Mother laughed a hollow kind of a laugh. "Oh, yes. If I'm not rested by now, I guess I never will be."

The silence hung between us. "What have you been doing, Dorrie?"

"Oh nothing much. I mean, there's not much to do. I mean . . ." I wanted to bite my tongue for saying that, but Mom didn't seem to hear.

I picked at my fingernails and wound the cord of the window shade around my index finger until it turned red and numb. I tried to look at my watch without looking at it. After all that had happened, there wasn't one single solitary thing I could think of to say. Then I remembered the cat.

Somehow I untangled myself from the window shade and the rocking chair. "Wait a minute, Mom. I'll be right back."

I ran down the hall to my room and got Fred's yellow cat. I'm not sure why except that it was something to do. Better than just sitting there. I went back and knelt on the floor next to the bed and put it on my mother's tray, right next to the empty coffee cup and the toast scraps.

"Oh, Dorrie, it's marvelous. Look, he's laughing at me." Mom held up the cat to the sunshine. Then she brought it close to her face and held it against her cheek. Her eyes looked through me—faraway.

Then she pushed the dishes aside and put the cat back on the tray. She looked right at me.

"Almost, Dorrie. I almost want to say 'Call Fred and we'll show him together—his cat.' " Her fingers rested on the yellow cat. "Almost. But I know I can't—ever again."

A feeling of cold horror took hold of me. For a terrible moment I knew what she meant. As if I could go across the hall and find Fred playing blocks or downstairs having milk and cookies.

"Mother, Fred's dead. He's dead and we buried him Monday. And he'll never see the cat. He's dead, Mom." And I felt as though it were years back and I was saying, "It's Piglet, Momma."

And I knew I was saying it as much for myself as for my mother.

Mom picked up the cat again, holding it carefully. "Poor Cat is for love," she said. I put my head down on the bed. Everything was quiet. My mother put her hand on my head, and it was a good feeling. "Yes, Dorrie," she said again, "Poor Cat is for love."

During the next few days Mother started coming downstairs more and more. First in her robe, then in clothes that hung. She looked pale and tired. She sat on the porch for hours at a time with a book in her hands, the pages never turned.

Friends came to call, and in the beginning

Grandma or Nellie, or even I, did most of the talking. Gradually my mother joined in.

After that there were short walks around the block or to a neighbors.

A trip to the drugstore for shampoo. A ride in the country—but I noticed that Grandma never took the back road, the one that went past the cemetery.

For some reason I couldn't understand, that awful, quiet town seemed to be making my mother whole again.

One day we walked over to the Bennett house. (I wondered how long it would be before anyone called it the Shafer house.) Mom had a measuring tape for the windows and a color chart of the paints and a little bit of interest on her face. Upstairs, in the room that was going to be mine, with the two steps down and its own den, she leaned on the windowsill and looked out.

"You do like it, Dorrie, don't you? The house and all?" I didn't answer at first. "Ye—es, the house is great, and so's the room." I couldn't say any more but it didn't seem to matter.

Mom was holding the paint chips against the wall. Her voice was forced. "What do you think? How about yellow? I think a studio couch in the den so you can bring your friends down from school. Maybe covered in orange or plaid."

Suddenly Mom sat down on the step. Her face was lined and tired. "Dorrie, I want you to know—

everything you did for Fred and the way you were with him that night—and for the yellow cat and a lot of things—well, I'm grateful."

It didn't seem right that my mother should thank me for anything. "But, Mom, I was horrible sometimes. Sometimes I didn't even like Fred, and the yellow cat was only because I was so awful to him the night he broke mine."

I stood by the door peeling scraps of blue wallpaper off the wall. Tatters of paper dropped onto the floor. I couldn't bring myself to say that though I missed Fred there had actually been times these last few weeks when I'd thought that life would be simpler without him. And there had been times when I'd awakened in the middle of the night with tears on my face because I missed him so. I could never tell my mother that. Instead, I pushed the chipped paper around the floor with my bare feet.

"But, Dorrie, nobody likes everybody all the time, or at least no one likes all the things a person does all the time. But maybe that's where love takes over. And no matter how you felt at times, you were good to Fred. You loved him, Dorrie, in spite of yourself."

I started to say something, but my mother put her hand up. "No more, Dorrie. I think I'm more tired than I thought. Let's just go home."

She took my arm and we started out of the room. The paint chips lay forgotten on the floor.

15

My brother was dead. Fred, who somewhere, long ago in my mind, was Fredlet, but would forever after be Fred. And in the weeks after the funeral—the weeks of my mother putting herself back together, and my father going back to New York to finish up at the office—and the weeks of aunts and cousins trying to make me part of their everyday lives—the weeks of still, motionless June heat—I did a lot of thinking.

Mostly I thought about Fred, with his little eyes and his runny nose and his Sears catalog and the way he bowed and talked to people. Fred really liked people. And thinking back on it, I guess people liked him. Except I didn't always. I remembered how I sometimes couldn't stand him, and how my mother said I loved Fred in spite of myself.

And I suppose she was right. I remembered how I sometimes looked in on him asleep, and how he held my hand in the ambulance, and how he broke the cat, and loved riding on buses.

I was glad Fred had been my brother. Had been, and still was, and always would be. Always would be in the way that everyone we've known is part of us. All tangled up in our lives. The way we're tangled up in theirs.

Then the thoughts got too big and I got my charcoals out and tried a few sketches, the first I'd done in a long time. At first my fingers felt stiff and the lines were awkward on the paper. But after a while it was all right again.

My father called and asked me to come to New York. He had finished work at the office and thought that between the two of us we could get the packing done in a couple of days. And my mother wouldn't have to make the trip.

Anyway, Ann and Pat had been calling the apartment and wanted to see me. And Guntzie had suggested that I pack the things I wouldn't need till winter and leave them in her storage cage in the basement so they'd be there in the fall.

I was excited about going—about having something to do. My mother was getting better. She kept the yellow cat on her dresser and sometimes when she passed it, she gave it a funny smile and a pat on the head. She seemed to belong in Tunbridge, as if all the aunts and uncles, great-aunts and cousins reached out to steady her. Soon my father would be there with her.

As for me—I wasn't sure. First came the next two years with Guntzie in New York to finish up at school and then art school. More than anything else I knew that. Then I wasn't sure. I couldn't see myself in Tunbridge forever. But I'd be coming back— not to stay—but coming back just the same. Because of my mother and father, and the aunts and the cousins and the uncles whose names I was only just beginning to learn.

Grandma and Aunt Nellie and my mother stood on the platform and we kept waving through the train window and mouthing words that nobody really understood. They felt they couldn't leave until the train started, and I felt I couldn't pick up a book while they were standing there.

Finally the train jerked backward—and then forward—and we all waved some more, and Grandma blew kisses.

By twisting around in my seat I could see them getting smaller and smaller as they walked toward the car.

My eyes stung. I leaned my head against the window and watched the railroad ties slip by underneath. I was sad and I was happy.

The train said, "Got your trunk—got your trunk." The train said, "Hate your brother—hate your brother—"
got your trunk—
got your trunk—
love your brother—

hate your brother—
got your trunk—
hate your brother—
love your brother—
love your brother—
love your brother—

all the way to New York.